THE TRUTH
—OF THE—
UNKNOWN
INTERPRETER

PAUL ARAMOUNI

Author ReputationPress®
Creativity & Branding

Author Reputation Press LLC
45 Dan Road Suite 5
Canton MA 02021
www.authorreputationpress.com
Hotline: 1(800) 220-7660
Fax: 1(855) 752-6001

Ordering Information:
Quantity sales. Special discounts are available on quantity purchases by corporations, associations, and others. For details, contact the publisher at the address above.

Printed in the United States of America.

ISBN-13:   Softcover   978-1-64961-135-2
           eBook   978-1-64961-136-9

Library of Congress Control Number: 2020917609

CONTENTS

ACKNOWLEDGMENTS

I WOULD LIKE TO express my deepest appreciation to all those who have provided me all the possibility to complete this report. Especially the main two people that have motivated and inspired me to have the ambition to write this book, my high school interpreters Vicky Long and Nichole Cohen. If it wasn't for those people and the dramatic high school life I have been through, this book would have never existed. Furthermore, I would like to acknowledge the group of people who had helped with different ideas, and whom have suggested the idea of writing this book, Mostly my mother Claudia Aramouni and multiple other people such as: Jared Palacios, and Jennifer Quintero. I would like to thank my team for the persistence of keeping the book to its highest point and making it as intriguing as possible. Adrianna Hernandez, Gloria Cifuentes and the head of the whole report Serah Ndinguri. I would like to thank everyone that has invested their time in helping me with this book and it would not have reached far without their help and opinions.

PREFACE

HUNDREDS OF THOUSANDS of people around the world have hearing disabilities and there is nothing wrong with that because most of the people are blessed with services that they are provided from their schools, government and different agencies. Furthermore, one of the best services a hearing impaired person could get are interpreters. The interpreters always provide attention and help translate what the speaker is saying. On the other hand, one of the less fortunate things that you'll rarely find in an interpreter is their lack of kindness. Some would be really rude, vile or could care less about what the client has to say or is going through.

I myself have been through many different kinds of interpreters in my school life. When I finally got to high school in West Palm Beach, Florida, I had two different interpreters. They both were the definition of good and evil out of all the interpreters. In the ninth grade, I felt like I had the best interpreter in the world. This interpreter was an angel to me and it felt like she was literally sent to me from heaven just to provide the best services to me. If you needed a friend, a person to borrow a dollar from or just an interpreter she would be the one to stand by you.

After a full amazing 2 year and a half something came up the interpreter had to go somewhere. She had to interpret for another client who just moved to American from a foreign country and he didn't really speak the languadge nor American Sign Language. She was the best person for the job and I do not blame her for being such a skilled and amazing interpreter. On the other hand, the other interpreter had shown me what the opposite of nice was. Don't get me wrong, she was very professional and always did the right thing regarding her job. Unfortunately her personality has shown nothing but pure annoyance, hatred, negligent, and repulsive remarks to the students and the staff. She would be really nice to the staff and then back stab them later and then talk about how awful my school was and would say ghastly things about my schools system, rules, learning environment and so much more.

I have kept it all a secret for four years until I finally said something. Little did I know I just fell into the hole a little deeper and no one did anything about it. Now the interpreter was angry at me which I completely understand. Which is why I am inspired enough to write this book about my most loving angel interpreter and the notorious other interpreter. This book is about the personalities and professionalism of interpreters.

INTRODUCTION

NE DAY AN interpreter in the name of Becky Malone was interpreting for a student named Henry Velovsky that she had always been interpreting ever since the students first day of school. During history class everyone was preparing for midterms and Becky gladly helped Henry. She was so sweet, kind, and also offered some notes she took. When lunch was over Henry was always so excited to get back to class and get ready for midterms with his study partner and interpreter, Becky. A substitute interpreter by the name of Jenese Motaire had to attend the study group and spent the rest of the day with Henry. When the last bell rang, Henry would always walk home with his three best friends. A couple of blocks down the road they heard a huge shriek and a really strong foul smell from a distance. Little does Henry know, he stumbled upon a carcass and found the head of his beloved interpreter Becky with the word carved "SWINE" on it.

CHAPTER 1

New Beginning

AUGUST 14, 2014. It was a rare sunny day in Fair Oaks, Oregon, which was in the northwestern United States amid extensive evergreen forests. Why was the city amid evergreen forests called fair oaks? No one was certain. Newly arrived from Russia was a teenage boy named Henry Velovski who had a hearing problem. Everyone in the beautiful foggy tall forests of Fair Oaks knew each other. It almost felt like it was a friendly safe environment for the people.

Yet there were some dark secrets that were kept in some of the deepest parts of the woods. There lies a myth that down in the deep woods where it grew pristine like northern red oak trees, there was an abandoned hospital for the insane people. Henry was always a curious and adventurous person. He walked out the back door of his house into the forest. Always loved to wander out into the forest and take a deep breath of nature while he thinks about how great his life is.

Then as Henry was listening to his music he saw an old man wandering around the forest in broad daylight. A car then pulled over and a man came out, he asked, "Hey, do you need help?" The old man then turns around to reveal blood smeared all over his mouth while yelling in some foreign language. The old man then starts sprinting to the driver, grabbing onto him. He then rips the collarbone of the poor innocent driver with his sharp teeth. A few moments later into that horrifying experience, Henry quietly started walking back to his house. Unfortunately, he accidentally stepped on a twig and it snapped. The cannibalistic man and Henry then made eye contact.

Henry's whole body froze. This man's horrifying look was petrifying. This white man, with a black outfit and leather jacket, shiny blue eyes, and bald. The warm air was coming out of the man's mouth as blood was dripping off from the sides of his chin. He roared out loud and while his life was on the line Henry ran for his life back to his house.

Henry stayed away from the woods and never spoke of the incident until it became breaking news on TV. He saw police officers knocking on doors to fill out reports of the mysterious incident that happened. It got to the point where Henry divulged with the two officers that came up to his door. When the police officers heard the news they simply just laughed and said, "Wow that's the best lead we have gotten all week!" Regardless of what Henry said he was just happy that he was alive and hopefully he would never see that old man who ate the poor driver.

On the first day of school at Dolce Gelato High, Henry takes his first steps into an all-hearing school whereas, back at home Henry was used to being in a deaf environment. He joined multiple clubs and organizations, as well as meet lots of different people with interesting appearances and cultures. Henry had always been at a school that had a program for deaf children but eventually, he got to the point where he got tired of seeing the same people for almost his whole life. Henry then moved to a hearing school, there would be children who would treat him really nice but some really vile. There would be times when Henry would go up to groups of kids at lunch or in class to ask if he could hang out with them, Most of the kids said no because he was too deaf to be around them and couldn't hang around with the "cool" kids. At times students would harass Henry saying "Hey, that person called you!" Or in games, they would say "Go, Henry! It's your turn!" When no one has said anything which humiliated Henry because people would laugh at Henry for doing something completely stupid or random when it was really the bullies that would play puppet with Henry. He strived to make new friends, but he would tend to be antisocial at times and a bit introverted around people. Although, there was this one particular person that always stood up for him and taught him some really good valuable life lessons, relationship advice and a tutor for most of his classes. She was basically a friend to him and that was his interpreter Becky Malone. Not only was Becky Malone a strong independent woman that thrived to help others but she was also an international contractor which basically means that she is a professional interpreter that would travel all around the world interpreting for world-famous pop stars to government agencies and to doctors offices to interpret from young kids to seniors. Becky also comes from a privileged family and society that would call them "The Malone's". They are a pretty powerful and important family. Becky recently just took a break from traveling from all over the world interpreting for philosophers, anthropologists, astronomers, and even mental health activists. After several years overseas, and reading through hundreds of different emails and messages from social media from family and friends saying that they missed her and wanted her to come back home, Becky then finally decided to take a huge break and just interpret locally in her hometown in Fair Oaks and her home school which is Dolce Gelato High School, home of the porcupines. Henry used to think that interpreters were the worst and the fact that he moved to America from Russia was just so that he could leave the deaf world and all the contracts he had regarding interpreters that had to be with him.

On the first week of school when Henry was struggling to make new friends and tried to speak the American language as much as he could but at the same time he was shy but outgoing at the same time. He was mostly happy because of the fact that he thought that he was in an interpreter free zone, but little did he know there was an interpreter named Becky Malone waiting for him in his first period class! Yet he tries to stay quiet throughout the entire time as much as he could. Consequently, he failed due to the attendance sheet that the teacher was going through. Once Becky spotted Henry in the far left side of the classroom, she then signed at Henry and said "Hey, Henry! My name is Becky Malone and I will be interpreting for you this year and hopefully four entire years!" "Yay! This should be fun!" Henry replied reluctantly and sarcastically. Henry always hated interpreters especially the interpreter that had been so mean and strict for almost his whole middle school life and even the students in his school hated his interpreter. Her name was Sunny Verruckt most kids would call her "witch lady."

When the interpreter caught Henry and introduced herself as the contractor interpreter for Henry Velovsky, he felt that his life was over, but at the same time tried his hardest to not expose himself and hid himself from his other classmates so that they wouldn't know he had a "babysitter" or a second "mom." When the first bell rang, Henry started seeing signs that he never saw in his life from any of his interpreters and it was a sign of independence! The interpreter would literally just walk away from Henry and just go to his next class as if it was her class. Normally the interpreter would just wait for Henry to finish packing and then would walk out Henry to his next class as if some secret service protecting the president's son. But the contractor interpreter started to make the deaf world a lot easier by giving Henry plenty of independence. When Henry was in middle school back in his country the interpreter would not only keep an eye over Henry throughout the entire school day, she also chased after kids that breathed funny. Sunny would threaten kids with many different huge demerits whenever she would assume they breathed funny. Or even when Henry tried to have a social life with his classmates, Sunny would take her twice-pierced snake tongue and yell at him to get back to the seat to do work regardless if he was done. Every day when Henry would come to school, Sunny would ask Henry if he had studied or done his homework with a scary look on her eye. Thankfully Henry was later then blessed with such an amazing interpreter like Becky in his high school. In Henry's computer science class, Becky would only interpret what the teacher said and then went back to her thing like reading magazines, talking to the teacher, or she would just go on her phone. Becky even allowed him to call her by her first name! By that time Henry had already loved her!

Becky was the complete opposite interpreter of what Henry had back in Russia at Honk-Son Christian Middle School. That interpreter was named Sunny Verruckt. Which Henry thought by far was the worst interpreter he had ever met and experienced. Sunny was ironically portrayed to be a nun but was always narcissistic, abrupt and always felt superior she literally never gave Henry liberty, space, patience nor to the other classmates. Becky was like the angel of all interpreters Henry has ever met along with his interpreters from elementary school and she wasn't even religious! At least that was what he thought, unlike that satanic nun Verruckt. Becky Malone had even helped Henry establish a sign language club for the entire school! Which not only helped the entire school become more knowledgeable with sign language but it also got Henry community service hours. Henry became known all over the entire school and got involved in so many activities while also having lots of fun nights with people! It was one of those impactful moments that Henry would never forget.

Whenever Henry needed a friend, tutor, a person to cry on, a person to keep company with, it would be Becky Malone. Even though all of the Henry's classes were so tedious, his interpreter would always find a make his classes joyful and cheerful.

After finals were over, Henry said goodbye to his friends, teachers, and interpreter even though he knows he will see his interpreter in his sophomore year. As soon as Henry rushed home he threw his backpack across his bedroom happily jumping on his bed. Henry was so excited to see what was in store for him and his family this summer. Later that evening, Henry had come down from his office to the dining table where everyone had been waiting for him to say grace before they ate a delicious meal. Henry has four siblings; John, Alex, Sam, and Megan. John is the oldest, Megan is the second oldest then Henry, then Alex then sam. The father's name is Jim and the Mother is Karen. "Alright everyone let's say grace before we eat," Jim started. "Dear Heavenly Father, I want to thank you for this food, our good Health, successes, our safety, home and help us all stay strong and guide us all to great paths, for we all can do things through Christ. In the name of Jesus, we pray," "Amen." Everyone replied. "So what are we doing this summer?!" asked Henry. " Well your mother and I are considering having us all take a week trip to Bora Bora and then the Maldives next! We would leave this Monday" Jim replied. The children all yelled with excitement, everyone talking at the same time. "Omigosh! I have so many things to do in such little time!" Megan shouted. " Um... dad, what about the private jet? Isn't it still in the hangar getting custom wrap?" John asked. " Yes it is still in the hangar getting custom wrapped, which is why we will be getting first class tickets to our regular flights to Bora Bora then rent a yacht to the Maldives." The family spends the rest of the night packing their bags for one of the best trips of a lifetime. The next morning Henry went out with his four best friends from school. They all went to the

"Washington Square Mall" and shopped there all day. As Henry was enjoying himself with friends, he thinks to himself, "Man, I wish they would come with my family and I to spend time with us in Bora Bora." After they all finished eating Henry said, " Hey! Why don't you guys come with me to Bora Bora for the next two weeks, and you guys could sleep over my house until the day of the trip?!" Henry's friends shouted yes while shocked with excitement. Henry's parents willingly agreed to allow his best friends to come to Bora Bora with his family only because Henry did really well in school. Summer went by and Henry has one of the best summers of his life, celebrating and traveling with friends and family going on vacations, sleepovers, restaurants and living the best time he could ever ask for. Henry and his family and friends flew back home and got ready for the New Year's celebration.

On the first day of Henry's sophomore year, Henry wakes up for school fully rested, happy, and prepared for his 10th-grade year with a whole outfit ready and hanged on his door with perfect shoes that matched, as well as being freshly groomed. Henry walked down the stairs as he saw his family all on the dining table eating and talking, which sparked a type of energy through his body that made him know that today was going to be a great day. A few moments later when Henry arrived to school and once he had gone into his first-period class which was biology, he had been sitting in the class and after a few minutes after the last bell Henry noticed that Becky was running a little late to class. When there was free time, Henry and Becky had the opportunity to talk. "So what did you do during the summer?" Henry asked. "Well, besides working with a few different jobs and helped my parents with their businesses, I went hiking with friends and family exploring the woods, partied a little bit went out with friends and that's about it!" Becky then suddenly starts to feel less fortunate. Henry then asks Becky, "What's wrong?" "This morning, before I drove to work I got this call from my boss from the agency and she said that I have to go to another job. A boy from Italy just moved here from Rome, and he barely knows any English but he is deaf and you will have another interpreter here that will interpret for you. Don't worry. She is really good and will be with you for the rest of the year." Henry, who was disappointed but understanding replied, "Awww, why can't the agency send that other interpreter instead of you? I wish you didn't have to go..." "I know, I'm sorry. I tried getting someone else to go but they said that the answer was final. I'm sure that new interpreter is not so bad." Becky replied. "I hope so!" Henry said, lightly laughing. Becky and Henry then go to the next class. Henry couldn't focus too well because he wouldn't stop thinking and worrying. "What if this becomes like Russia all over again? I really don't want to suffer like the way I did throughout my middle school years back home. Hope I get someone as good as Becky!" Henry said to himself. He proceeds to attempt to focus as he awaits for the mysterious interpreter to come by. Thirty minutes had gone by, which was almost time for the bell to ring to his next class. Henry was so bored of the lecture so he then decided to take a nap. Shortly after, however, Henry awoke to the sound of a loud banging on the door of the classroom. He started getting sad and sucked up his tears and knowing that whatever was coming through that door was going to be his new interpreter until he graduates. As the teacher had open the door Henry had felt a cold chill from the hallways and started getting goosebumps. A short mysterious crone woman comes in and said to the teacher "I am looking for Henry Velovski." The whole thing sounded so ominous like it came out of a "Jason - Friday the 13th" movie. She had a deep scratchy voice and goes by the name of Jenese Motaire. When she had asked for Henry Velovsky at that moment, the whole room went dark. The whole class looked at him and felt frightened that something menacing would happen. At first, Henry though he was dreaming, pinching himself in hope that he would wake up. But then realizes that everything was real and that his world was about to change. After Becky introduced Henry and the interpreter, Becky said to not worry and if the interpreter was ever mistreating Henry then to call Becky then she would go beat up the interpreter but of course, she was joking. As Henry waved goodbye to Becky walking to her car through the window, the new interpreter behind him says "We're going to have so much fun together this year and forever, I promise you." She pressed her head against Henry slithering her tongue away at Henry's ear, softly putting her long curvy dirty hands on Henry's shoulders. With Henry's eyes covered in tears and through the blurriness which looked like there were maggots crawling through her nails and around her fingers, Henry shrieked as he ran straight to his JROTC class.

As Henry disturbingly goes through the day with the most disgusting, ghastly and nerve-racking interpreter ever as he deeply inside hoped that Becky Malone would change her mind and come back the next day. But then he knew he had to be realistic and face new changes. When it was finally almost time for lunch, as Henry was getting ready to bolt out the door to get as much breath and freedom he could from his new interpreter, Jenese said "Hey, why don't we leave class a little bit early, and you could beat all the other kids at line in the cafeteria?" "Sounds good!" Henry replied. He then starts to change his mind about Jenese and thought maybe she wasn't too bad after all. But at the same time Henry still stayed very alert for he knew that she shouldn't be trusted. When Henry had gone to lunch he talked with his friends about the worst week that he was having so far. After lunch, Henry went to his the next class which was history, waiting for Jenese to help him with his history notes and prepare for the midterm. After waiting for a while, Jenese comes into the class with a giant bandage on her arm and says that she got cut by glass when it fell in the teachers planning room. Henry replied loudly with a smirk on his face, "You sure it wasn't a knife fight over someone's lunch you ate?" Even though no one was there to see it happen she claimed to have bandaged herself and cleaned the area spotless with no one there. Everyone seemed a little suspicious but still proceeded on with the day. When the last bell rings to go home, Henry felt so energetic and ready for his history exam next week. He bursts out the door seeking the beautiful freedom away from that interpreter as he joyously skips towards his house. As Henry gets through the middle of the parking lot he notices glass everywhere and sees Becky's car with the engine running as the driver's seat window was shattered and the whole car smelled like bleach as if someone wanted to clean up what no one was supposed to see and on the floor there was a note and had a smudge of blood on it! The note read: "HELP!!!"

CHAPTER 2

The Passing of Becky Malone

ONE WEEK LATER, on a Sunday morning, it was a cold, gloomy, sorrow day in the middle of December just a couple days after Christmas. Hundreds if not thousands of people families, police officers, hounds and so much more law enforcement searched and searched until the point where the case had to give up and stay a mystery. Becky Malone's family had a funeral and Henry had attended. A few hours go by and in the distance, Henry sees a mysterious looking person. It seems to be a woman with a black cloak with a black bowler hat with a red feather on top and was carrying a mysterious crow-headed cane. The person also happened to have a huge sized vulture on the right shoulder and it looked so fierce as it devoured its breakfast which seemed like an opossum. The woman throws a smirk and at Henry then chuckles as the vague mysterious woman vanishes on the horizon. There was also another shadow figure behind a tree but it looked so peculiar and it seemed that if that person was holding some sort of sickle and it seemed something was impaled onto it.

Once the funeral was over and after everyone pays their respects to Becky Malone's casket, everyone goes to the parents of Becky's home for a gathering while share loving memories that each family member and friend had with Becky. Even Henry's family had attended the funeral and the house gathering. Becky's parents was one of the richest families in the small town of Fair Oaks. The Malone's were so rich that they had their own funeral in their backyard with over 695 acres worth of land. It was so foggy and scary that people thought it was downright creepy. But they reluctantly wanted to go to the funeral at the same time because they felt bad for the death of Becky Malone.

When school started the following week, Henry and his friends walked towards the gates of the school but they stopped upon on the parking lot in front of the school campus. There were still lots of CSI agents, some Forensic scientists, sheriffs, K9's and hounds. Meanwhile the whole city of Fair Oaks was trying to solve the mysterious tragic incident of how Becky Malone disappeared on broad daylight. Days go by the parents start to see that the results weren't progressing any faster. Luckily the father who knew almost all of the population in the state of Oregon was able to get in touch with the best law enforcement in the state. The Father's name was Clyde Malone, he owns the Portland trail blazers NBA basketball team, half of Nike and is the chairman of T-Mobile headquarters. One of his good buddies was a detective and they parted ways after college, 20 years ago. But they still always kept in touch. As the retired detective William Henshaw Paine was sipping a martini while lying in the beautiful beach in the Maldives with his wife and children, he received a call from one of his best friends, Clyde. "Hey" William answers while expressing condolences to Clyde's daughter and how she was beautiful talented woman who didn't have the right to die in such a young age. "I know. Thanks, bro. Really appreciate it. Listen, I could really use your expertise. I know that you resigned and having a wonderful time with your wife and kids but I could really use your help for this one last final favor."

After William packed his bags, him and his family rushed back home to help solve the investigation of the disappearance of Becky

Malone. William Henshaw Paine was one of the top detectives around. He was an expert which was why he was popular for his work. He grew up in the suburbs of Lake Oswego, Oregon, a son of a successful but corrupted Marines veteran. William was inspired by his father to study criminal justice while also studying psychology and legal studies.

Once William sees Henry all gloomy and hopes that his best friend interpreter would be found soon, he walks over to Henry and says "I will do everything in my power to help find your interpreter wherever she is but I cannot guarantee you that she's alive." Henry wipes his tears and bravely tries to continue on to his school day while unenthusiastically trying to stick with his new weird interpreter that he never felt comfortable with. Jenese was always weird, smelled weird, and whenever she smiled and when you would look closely between her black and yellow teeth you could almost see something crawling in there like a cricket or beetle. She also acted funky, always seemed like she was hiding something, her eyes would always twitch every two minutes and it was the most disturbing figure ever. Yet Jenese still always tried to become the better version of Becky. Not only does she try to be his interpreter but also wanted to have a mutual relationship with him.

Jenese used to talk about how her husband died over a decade ago. But she prefers not to talk about it. One of Henry's best friends, Tristan, was the head leader of the group and also is a linebacker on the football team. Another of Henry's best friends, Ben, is the battalion commander of the JROTC program as well as the president of the honors society. Henry's third best friend, Elizabeth, is a soccer player and Susan, the last of the friend group, is a cheerleader and also the volleyball captain. Every time when Henry has P.E or PT for JROTC the interpreter would always stay indoors. Henry thought it was shockingly peculiar that she could not be outside or even drink orange juice considering the fact that it has vitamin C in it. When the last bell had rung then the group of best friends started home. As they were walking home, they were talking and laughing, then all of a sudden there was a huge shriek from one of the neighbors. Henry and his friends ran to see what was going on. That vile smell was almost similar to what henrys current interpreter would smell sometimes, like something died or was spoiled and spilled all over her. Tristan was daring Henry to go see what was in the dumpster but the girls were trying to convince him not to do something that dangerous. Giving into the pressure, however, he slowly started to approach the dumpster whilst his heart was pumping rapidly. Henry stumbles upon two separate black bags and felt a very liquidity substance and saw that it was blood! His heart was beating rapidly, he reluctantly opens the bag and sees a torso with a decapitated head. Frightened by his findings, he jumps back and slams his head on the wall behind him. While uneasy from the pain, Henry's friends find the bag and open it. Now everyone sees the head of Becky Malone, along with the word "SWINE" carved on her forehead! Henry and his friends shriek and ran home to immediately tell their parents about what they saw.

CHAPTER 3

The Rumor

THE NEXT MORNING, Henry felt traumatized from what had happened the previous day. He seemed depressed and monotonous as if the image he saw sucked the happiness out of his soul. Henry's mother had been calling around to see how to help Henry, as hurt as he was from seeing his favorite interpreter beheaded. One person she stumbled upon was a doctor named Shannon Alvarez.

Dr. Shannon Alvarez had recently resigned from The Cottage Springs Hospital in Medford, Oregon. That city had some of the most notorious, nefarious and wicked minded psychopaths, serial killers,etc. Most of those people dealt with schizophrenia, PTSD, dementia and so much more. Dr. Alvarez just recently started working locally at a small private clinical office.

Dr. Alvarez also deals with children struggling with emotional pain from divorces, bullies at school and also helps with traumatic events. What Henry had witnessed was a motive of a narcissistic serial killer that premeditated the murder based on what detective William has documented in the records. After a month of hardcore thorough sessions, he was allowed to go to school. When Henry went into the gates of the school the whole school went silent and looked at Henry like he was some outsider from another dimension.

In the early springtime, the JROTC program was having a military ball in a rather lavish hotel on the coast of Oregon.

Ben invited Henry to the military dance with Susan as Henry's escort. As Henry gets to the party at the hotel, he starts to socialize with the other party members. The one thing that he felt most uncomfortable with was the fact that people kept asking what really happened on that one afternoon that he found the dead body. He would just said "Hey, really now. I'm fine and I just want to relax and have a good time with you guys." Hours go by, people get their pictures taken, people were passed out on the floor, and Henry was having the best time of his life with Susan. Moreover, the party was not over yet! Tristan who was still hyped from the party and had decided to make an after party. He booked a vacation home at Cannon Beach and about half of the party had went when the ball was over. At midnight, Tristan, his friends, and a bunch of other people were partying, playing beer pong, smoking narcotics, having sex and drinking in the after party. Henry was having a blast and felt so replenished that his friends were getting the horrific images off his mind. Henry steps outside to take a breath from the wildness. Over the distance he spots Susan sitting around the fire pit along the shore with beautiful quiet waves and the full moon shining on the endless sea. As the people roast marshmallows, making s'mores, people talking and singing, Henry joins the club and starts talking to Susan. After a while, Susan gets up and holds on to Henry's hands as they walk onto the shore. They then lay down to they watch the beautiful gleaming stars and the wishing star flying by, She leans over him and says "I wanted to tell you that I will always be here for you whether you did something stupid or not. I just want you to know that you are never alone and I will always be there next to you. What you did in that neighborhood was stupid and you should have never done that just to impress your friends or when someone dares you to do something stupid." Henry apologizes, then goes for a kiss.

At dawn the next morning, Henry wakes up to see Susan sleeping next to him. "How did I ever meet such a beautiful, mesmerizing, smart, athletic girl?" He thinks to himself. Moments later he sees a strange shadowy figure through the foggy sea and it seemed as if a person was floating towards the shore on a raft with a long edged sickle. It seemed to have on a long black cloak. Henry knew it was the same image he saw from the funeral he freaked out. "Susan! Susan!, we have to go it's here!" yells Henry. "What is?" Susan replies. "It is the monster from the funeral! It's here!" Henry says. The shadowy figure gets to shore faster and the two start to hyperventilate. But as the raft got closer, you could see Tristan jumps of it, wearing a raincoat and had a fish hook with a fishing net. "Hey guys, brought some breakfast!" Tristan yells. Ben runs outside and asks "Hey, what happened? I heard screaming. Are you guys okay?" "Yes, it's just the nightmares that's all" Henry replied. Everyone goes to the patio to eat breakfast and talk while watching the beautiful sunrise on the beach. "So what happened last night? Are you guys talking now?" Tristan asks Henry and Susan. They both stayed silent while eating.

When school started the following week, everyone started to respect Henry a little bit more, even though there have been some people that would pick on him because of what had happened. There had also been some rumors on the "Henry, Susan, Situation" that had happened on the weekend of the after party in Cannon Beach. As the day goes by, Principal Garrett calls in Henry into the main office. Henry steps in and sees detective William in the room. Detective William starts asking him some questions regarding the incident that had happened in the neighborhood. The detective also showed Henry some of the results that they have found in the dumpster and the murder weapon that was found on the grass a couple feet away from the dumpster. It happened to be a sickle and it had some sort of bull symbol on it like from a religious cult. When Henry saw the hook, it shocked him so badly he literally saw it from the funeral he was at and thinks that someone is out to get him. Detective William wasn't so sure about where the symbol had come from since he mostly worked with cases in the U.S or in some parts of Europe. Although he knew the perfect person for the job so he recommended that Henry went to detective William's sister, Dr. Shannon. Henry then goes to the psychologists office after school for his session. Henry talks about what he had done during school or in his free time ever since his last appointment with Dr. Shannon a month ago. He also talks about how he went to the military ball from his schools JROTC program and then went to the after party and saw a crazy shadowy figure but it was only his head playing tricks with him. Afterwards, Henry then talks about the little meeting he had with Detective William and brings up this picture that he saw on the file from the crime scene. Dr. Shannon was very shocked and confused because she had been studying this symbol for almost 30 years of her career and had said to him: "This symbol originated in Rome but was mostly worshipped by a family in Russia. They were the Verruckt family. This religion goes all the way back to 300 B.C. This religion participated in one of the most insane satanic rituals that these families have performed and they would take people or animals and sacrifice themselves"

In a pit, a group of people in black robes would be surrounded by this sacrificial contestant and worship the bull. Dr. Shannon had never seen this type of work ever in U.S soil and it seems as if this person is back in action because it's been 10 years. She had seen this case regarding this symbol in Zimbabwe, Africa where there were multiple wild animals carved with the symbol of the bull god in Wicca and went by the name of "Dionysus." He is the ancient God of fertility, the God of forest, the flock, field and also of the hunt. After the informative session, Henry then goes home to study this ancient cult and why they would come out of nowhere or what this even had to do with Becky Malone. Since the incident, Henry would get these nightmares from the past and so many different flash forwards.

Henry tries out for the basketball team so he can stay active during the day to keep him busy from other things. After school, Susan and Henry go out to eat. As they talk about their days, Henry mentions something about what detective William was talking to him about regarding the murder weapon that the police had found. Henry tells her the whole history about that bull and what it represents and how insane narcissistic psychopaths follow this ritual. As Susan laughs she then looks at the picture and opens her mouth in pure shock. "One of the girls in my cheerleading team has that symbol engraved on her purse!" Susan said frighteningly.

CHAPTER 4

The Change

ENRY AND SUSAN were talking about the marked symbol that this girl and as it turned out, she was a Motaire! The following day, when Henry went to school, eating lunch with his friends, a squad of girls and some of the jocks from the football team burst through the entrance of the cafeteria. Henry spots a girl who seems to be the kingpin of her group. "Who is that girl?" Henry whispers to his friends. "That's Victoria Motaire, the captain of the cheerleading and dance team!" Susan then replies. She then talks about how Victoria uses her wealth to control what people do and bullies other people who don't "respect" her.

The linebacker of the team was going out with her at the time. He was one of the biggest pranksters in the whole school. Him and his football teammates were so mean to anyone that would stand in their way. When Victoria had heard about the incident involving Henry's interpreter, she felt no sympathy for his beloved "bodyguard." Then as Eric would pass by him in the hallways he would say "Hey, where is your bodyguard?" as the whole team would laugh. This time, Henry got so mad that he threw a punch at him only to get thrown down and beat up, followed by a warning not to mess with him ever again or he would face even worse repercussions. Henry then throws the middle finger while smiling with pride as

Eric throws a smirk as if he knew what nefarious things he would do to Henry.

Henry's friends help him up and walks him home after school. "Are you okay?!" one of the friends ask. "I'll be fine." Henry replies with a groan. The following morning when henry went to school, he felt so melancholy he would most of the time sit by himself and eat by himself. He could care less when people pick on him because all he could ever think about was stopping the bullies from bullying him and hoping that detective William finds the murderer of his beloved interpreter. The bell rang to go to the next class and a couple of feet away from the locker room, there seemed to be a huge amount of people talking. Henry and Susan walk through the crowd wondering what in the world was going on. They saw animal blood all over the locker and it said "YOU'RE NEXT" with a red feather on the floor in front of the locker. "That is the same red feather I saw from that mysterious person in the funeral!" Henry thought to himself. Later that day, Henry saw Eric in the courtyard chilling with his friends. Out of nowhere, he became filled with rage and charged towards him. Eric was throwing punches as they were yelling at each other. Security guards came rushing in, each grabbed one person and took them to the principal's office. Mr. Garrett was really infuriated with the fighting that was happening on the campus and then the principal's secretary pulled up the clip of the time when Henry's locker was being vandalized, Eric was the one that got caught. The principal took Eric off the football scholarships that he received for college and got suspended from school for the whole month. Henry only got suspended for three days. While Henry was alone at home, he hears barking in the backyard from his dogs. A couple minutes later of trying to get the dogs to shut up. Henry then goes outside in the chilly weather and calls the dogs inside for dinner. He then sees a huge light far into the woods and a couple of torches as the light fades away into the distance. Henry rushes to his room and calls Tristan and Ben about what he saw in the woods. He urgently tells them to come to his house to explore the woods in his backyard and find out where the mysterious torches were heading to. A little over an hour when it was clear and dark outside with the full moon was shining over the woods, the boys finally arrived on their bikes. They had originally sneaked out their houses through their bedroom windows. "Hey, where is Susan and Elizabeth?" Tristan asks Henry. "They are at the mall hanging out with friends.They are going to have a sleepover this weekend," he replied.

The boys walk through the creepy woods with their flashlights looking for the fire that Henry had saw. While looking, the group started talking about the military ball as well as the after party at the beach house. "So... you and Susan are now official now, Henry?" Tristan asks. "We are not official yet. All we did was kiss." " I bet you guys smashed considered the fact I saw you guys sleeping together outside in the beach!" Ben exclaims. The boys started laughing only to be interrupted by a strange fire pit they noticed in the distance. Henry tells them to be quiet as they crouch down, ever so slowly reaching the spot of the fire pit. While hiding behind a bush, they see a group of people in black cloaks surrounding the fire.

The group of mysterious cloak wearing gatherers take off their hoodies only to reveal that it was some people from the cheerleading squad and football team including Victoria and Eric! A couple of yards over there was another person that was much scarier. They were huge and whoever it was had a red cloak with feathers and some sort of cloth mask complete with a dunce cap. As the peculiar figure got closer, something huge that they were holding became more and more prominent. It was a boar head and it was dripping blood from its mouth. Whatever ritual was going on, the boys didn't like it. The red cloaked person drops the boar in front of the fire pit where the it was engulfed in flames which soon enough cause the flames to burst into an even larger flame. "That must have been the blood that they used on my locker." Henry whispers to the rest of the group. Everyone from the cloaked group pulls out their daggers and they perform their ritual cult. Ben takes out his phone to record what was going on. At the end of the ritual the group cuts the limbs from the other half of the boar's body that was left aside all the while worshipping some demigod called "Dionysus" with their hands raised up. Henry was so frightened that he closed his eyes until they were done. Then the person in the red cloak took of its mask and it just so happened to be none other than Jenese Motiare, Henry's current interpreter! "We have to go… now!" Tristan whispers to the group. But of course, as the group tried to sneak away, Ben steps on a twig. The snap of a twig caused everyone from the fire pit to look up and saw a group of boys. "STOP THEM!" Jenese yells. The boys all ran for their lives and didn't stop until they got home. The three boys got to Henry's house panting and catching their breath. His mother then comes to the kitchen where she sees the boys and asks "What's wrong? Why are you guys out of breath?" Henry then tells her, catching his breath "We were chased by wolves. Can Tristan and Ben stay over for the night?" "Sure that's fine." she answers. As Henry sets up the guest rooms Tristan asks "So what is going to happen when we get back to school on Monday?" to which Henry replies with "I don't know. I don't think anyone really saw us, especially Jenese. But we will definitely take this footage to detective Williams because it seems like it has the same motive for what happened to Becky."

Meanwhile on the other side of town, Susan, Elizabeth and two other girls had a sleepover for the weekend at Bethany's house. They had all met from the soccer team since most of them were soccer players.

Elizabeth had thought of this idea of hanging out at the mall and having a slumber party at Bethany's house to catch up on things that had happened over the past couple of weeks. After a long day of shopping at the mall, the girls decide to stop by the cafe they usually go to. "So what happened on the night on the after party? Ben said you and Henry were under the stars on the beach kissing." Elizabeth asks. "We just talked and somehow we just happened to kiss and cuddle for the night and then I fell asleep in his arms on his warm strong body. We are still talking but are not sure if we are official yet." Susan said. Elizabeth then talks about how she has a crush on Tristan and they have been talking for several weeks now. The girls gossip all night about boys and sports while eating dinner and drinking frappuccinos. The next morning when all the boys were sleeping, Tristan decided to pull a prank on Henry while he was still sleeping. Tristan borrowed a red robe from Henry's mom and used some red clothing to make the outfit similar to what he and his friends had witnessed the other night in the woods. Tristan pokes Henry to wake him up. Henry kicks and screams out of fear only to realize that it was just his friends under the cloak. After breakfast, the boys quickly started heading to school.

The girls woke up they all felt so happy and well rested as they talked and got ready for school. Elizabeth had made breakfast then everyone went to school. When the squad met each other in the courtyard. Henry had told the news and the girls were in shock. he then told them the plan of what was going to happen next. A few minutes after the conversation was over, Jenese was spotted on the hallway and she walks pass the group to class while giving them a cold stare.

CHAPTER 5

Jenese Motaire

THE FOLLOWING WEEK, Henry went to see Dr. Shannon for the last few times before he is officially done for the season. When walking by the hallways he notices his interpreter from school near the exit. Henry stops by her and asks very nervously, "Hey Jenese... What are you doing here?" Jenese replies with, "Oh, I came to see how you were doing in your sessions with Dr. Shannon. But the secretary said that Dr. Shannon is in break room having lunch so I had to go. So how are your sessions going? Are you okay?" As Jenese kept asking Henry nonstop questions, he answered them all but it felt tedious to him so he says "I'm fine really, thanks for checking up on me, now if you will excuse me, I am late to my session." They then part ways as they wave bye to each other.

Henry walks into the lobby. He then asks the secretary if Dr. Shannon was available. As the secretary calls Dr. Shannon's office in the intercom she then points to her office giving the "Okay" sign saying that Dr. Shannon just finished her lunch break and is in her office. Henry then walks in to the office, greets Dr. Shannon, and shows the pictures and evidence of what happened in the woods that night. Dr. Shannon noticed the motives of how the ritual was portrayed and the symbols with costumes. "Wow! This is interesting! I have seen a similar case to this before but I know a colleague who is more skilled in this. He is specialized in cases on religious cults and studies human behaviors. Her name is Dr. Yuri Zhivago She is from japan and has studied so many different rituals, cults, and religious beliefs from so many different countries going from Japan, Russia, Ukraine, some countries in Africa, Iceland and multiple countries in Europe." Dr. Shannon tells Henry. Dr. Shannon starts coughing throughout the conversation. Her coughs started getting worse and then Henry noticed blood on her hands. "Are you okay, Dr. Shannon?" "I'm fine" Dr. Shannon says. Moments later as Dr. Shannon was talking about her good friend doctor that would be a much greater help for Henry regarding the pictures that he had shown. Dr. Shannon started slurring in speech and she was starting to feel hot and sweaty. As Henry starts replying back about how cool it would be to get to meet Dr. Yuri, Dr. Shannon started to hear a loud screeching ring and she fell back and landed onto the floor. She heard the echoing sounds of Henry shouting "Help! Help! Someone call 911!" Henry pleads to Dr. Shannon to stay awake with him as she saw four heads swaying saying "Everything is going to be okay"

The secretary rushes to the door and directs the paramedics to where Dr. Shannon's office was. They lifted her onto a wheeled stretcher and rushed to the hospital. Shortly after, the police officers started investigating the premises, putting up caution tapes and looking for evidence of what had happened to Dr. Shannon. Henry sits down and takes a deep breath to try to process what had just happened. Henry then notices the tea cup that Dr. Shannon was drinking from before all of this and reaches for it to throw it away. Upon picking it up, he sees some strange black powder which was peculiar to him because he knew that Shannon only drinks green tea. While inspecting the cup, he spotts the bull symbol on the bottom of the cup! Henry silently gasps then puts the cup into his bag. He then went to the secretary to gather information of the whereabouts of Dr. Yuri Zhivago. Dr. Yuri lived in her parents

Japanese style villa, almost in the middle of nowhere at the northern parts of Oregon

As Henry pulls up through the gated driveway he passes by a beautiful cherry blossom trees and many different extravagant plants. He got to the door and knocked. A few moments later a woman opens the door and Henry said, "Hi, I am looking for Dr. Yuri Zhivago." "Who's asking?" said Dr. Yuri. Henry explains that Dr. Shannon referred him to her and that she will be a greater use to help with the case that he is trying to solve.

Dr. Yuri and Henry start walking and talking about the case at hand. However, Henry found himself in awe by the arts and ancient artifacts the family had in the household. Soon after, Henry and Dr. Yuri pass by a dojo where Henry was intrigued as to how there were hundreds of people training and fighting in combat with multiple different weapons in such a small space. When the two reach the Zen Garden, they sit by the Koi Pond to which Henry then proceeds to talk about what had happened to Dr. Shannon. Upon hearing the news, Dr. Yuri gasped. "Is she going to be ok?" All Henry could do was look down slowly with no hope in his mind. One of the house maids came to the room at that moment to serve them tea. Henry takes a sip and his face instantly lights up. "Wow, this is delicious! Where do you get this tea from?" Henry immediately asked. Dr.Yuri then gets up to show Henry the backyard that spanned hundreds of acres, all with lots of bundles of fruits and vegetables.

"All of the tea is made here and they could be used for healing or poisoning. Some of them can be cured but not all of them." Yuri said. Yuri was not sure why Dr. Shannon was poisoned, but she said that one of the main reasons why that ritualistic cult would do such a thing is because they either wanted to get revenge or they are out to get you and the ones you love. Henry then starts to gather all the pieces of what has been happening to him starting from the prank that Eric, the football player, had done thinking no one saw him.

Henry then asks "Do you think my interpreter Jenese is out to get me? Maybe that's why she possibly killed Dr. Shannon; so that I would stop the investigation of the murder of Becky Malone!"

Suddenly, there was a small growl among the bushes. Dr. Yuri tells Henry to be quiet and stand still. He then started to have palpitations and tried not to panic. He decided to quietly walk back but accidentally stepped on a dead plant causing it to make a very audible snap sound. Not even a second later, a wolf jumped out of the bushes and almost takes a bite out of Henry! Yuri then swings a stick at the wolf but it was strong. As they were struggling to take down the wolf, one of the archers from the roof had spotted the threat. The archer takes out the bow and arrow and pulls its lethal arrow back. After the archer had let go of the arrow, it flew so fast that it was able to impale the wolf's heart. Henry then looks back on the rooftop and sees a stunning girl who looked as beautiful as the sun sets behind her in the background. "Who is she?" Henry asks in awe. "That is my youngest sister. Her name is Elena. She will be joining us for dinner, if you would like to join."Dr. Yuri says.

Around dusk when the rest of the family was there, they all talked and laughed. No one talked about the case because Henry knew that the social environment would turn around and he didn't want to ruin everyone who was already having a good time.After a while, Henry walks through the hallways, he then spots beautiful Elena by the docks near the Koi pond, gazing upon the moonlight and stars. He walked up to Elena confidently, but was deathly nervous inside. A conversation starts and later on Elena asks, "Do you think you would ever train here at the dojo to protect yourself from that crazy psycho?" They both laughed and Henry replied with, "Sure, why not?" After they both part ways, Dr. Yuri stopped Henry at the door and then offers him to stay in for the night. "Oh, no. I shouldn't."Henry says. "It's too dangerous at night and you might get attacked by the wolves again or worse. You will leave first thing tomorrow morning, Come I will call your parents to let them know." Dr. Yuri finishes. One of the house maids then sets up one of the guest rooms for him to sleep in.

A couple hours later before dawn the front door of Henry's bedroom starts to open and he gasped in fear. Elena shushes him with her finger pressing on her lips and she crawls in his bed with him. "What are you doing?" Henry asks. Elena only replies with, "Just be quiet and relax." Elena throws in a kiss then they slept together.

CHAPTER 6

The Malone's

THE NEXT MORNING Henry wakes up and sees that Elena was gone but then finds her standing by the balcony enjoying a beverage. Henry gently holds Elena into her arms and enjoys the beautiful morning breeze of the horizon. Birds were chirping and the warriors in the dojo training. "Whatever happened last night should remain a secret that no one can ever know about." Elena says. Henry agrees but then replies saying, "Last night, before I could stop you, I was going to tell you that I am in a relationship..."

At breakfast, Dr. Yuri asks Henry "So, did you sleep well last night?" "Yes, although just a little tired from that house tour." Henry replies. "Right...." Elena says awkwardly. Henry was doing a terrible job keeping last night a secret because everyone was confused by his response.

While the family finished up breakfast and finished cleaning up, Henry gets a text message from his friends telling him to meet them at Tristan's house for a cool announcement. Henry thanks Dr. Yuri for the stay and the amazing breakfast and says bye to everyone. He leaves out the front door and makes way to the chauffeur on the driveway. Elena stops Henry as she rushes through the door and says, "Will we see each other ever again?" Henry replies with, "We can hang out together with my friends or just us if you want?" Elena then confirms and hugs Henry as he leaves for Tristan's house.

When Henry had arrived at Tristan's house, he noticed his mom's car and a Black SUV. After Henry presses the doorbell then as Tristan opens the door then sees all his friends, his mom, and Detective William with a file. Henry asks peculiarly "Hi... what is going on?" Henry's mother tells him that detective William has some news regarding the case. Detective William then said, "Henry, I got the results from both of the crime areas and what the investigators found out was that there were multiple footprints. The sizes were small, the way the glass was shattered seemed reckless, and there seemed to be mascara left on the door, which was most likely from the suspect since Becky Malone was not wearing make up at the time. The other set of footsteps was under a huge tree, which was strange because the suspect had the same motive on the other crime scene near the dumpster. The investigators claimed that the suspect who always hid among the shadows had lupus, due to the burnt skin marks pealed of the body due to the sun light."

Henry asks, "So there are now two suspects running around the states that have murdered the interpreter?!" The detective says, "Unfortunately, yes." Detective William then wraps up the meeting and proceeds with further investigations. Henry then stays over at Tristan's house to spend the night. "So, how was the place of this new doctor you saw?" Tristan asks Henry; Henry talks about how amazing the house was, the people, and how there was a dojo filled with cool ninja and jujitsu warriors. Henry also described many of the beautiful lavish gardens, Zen garden, movie areas and even a gaming area. Tristan wished he had gone to see.

The next morning, Tristan had an amazing idea that everyone goes out and spend the entire day at the water park. In the meantime, while everyone was enjoying their breakfast.

Henry talks about the investigation that detective William was talking about yesterday. Maily, about how one of the suspects has lupus. One time when Jenise was outside for more than two minutes her skin started to turn red then some skin parts of her body would boil then peel off as if she had leprosy. Tristan says, "Most students hate your interpreter and even the staff." The boys laugh as they agree. Later in the afternoon when everyone was having a blast in the Water Park, Susan and Henry enjoy themselves and talking about how they missed each other. A little later in the day Henry receives a text from the detective saying there was a funeral that was happening the next day for Dr. Shannon. Everyone goes on the following morning. Henry then sees Mr. Shannon, the husband of Dr. Shannon. Mr. Shannon looks at Henry with a very villainous look.

CHAPTER 7

The Widow

D R. SHANNON'S BURIAL ceremony was one of the saddest events Henry had attended the whole year. He found out that she was married, with two young children. The children, who had been very close to their mother, could not understand why their mother had to die. Their father was overwhelmed with grieve and he avoided to talk to anyone who approached him with stories about his deceased wife. Mr. Shannon kept throwing Henry a hateful look and all this time Henry was dying to approach him and clear things with him. He felt that Mr. Shannon blamed him for the death of his wife. When Henry got the chance, he approached the widower Mr. Shannon and tried to initiate a conversation. "Hello, Mr. Shannon? Your wife was such a kind soul. I have her to thank for my better mind state." Henry started but then the widower rudely intercepted, "Yeah? You might as well follow her and thank her in hell or wherever!" Henry was puzzled and he slowly walked away into the crowd. As he searched for a lone spot to sit, he notices another woman watching him from the crowd like her plus one or something. He felt scared, especially since he suspected that she had something to do with poisoning Dr. Shannon.

Henry finally managed to sneak out of her watch. He found a rock far from the graveyard and sat down, getting lost behind the mourning crowd. When the crowd started clearing, he noticed Jenese talking to Mr. Shannon. Henry found this particularly weird because he remembered how rude Mr. Shannon was towards him. He wondered how Jenese could have possibly managed to engage him and what they were talking about. He decided to approach the two and when he got there, Mr. Shannon was in a surprisingly good mood. He did not even notice he was talking to Henry when he blurted out "My son, Jenese here was just telling me about the great business deals we are about to make after this. My wife died for a good cause." Henry felt weirdly uncomfortable and he had to excuse himself. He could not help but wonder how Mr. Shannon could possibly be so happy about his wife's death when a while ago he acted like his whole world had just caved in. Something did not just add up. He slithered through the crowd and started walking home, confused which direction his investigations should take.

Initially, Henry was positive that Jenese had poisoned Dr. Shannon's tea but now he was confused, trying to understand what part Mr. Shannon had played in his wife's death. "Did Jenese follow him to the doctor's office or was she directed here by Mr. Shannon?" He thought to himself. He also wondered why the two seemed so close as if they had been acquainted before. The new turn of events made him start questioning everyone and everything. His investigation mission was more challenging and the clear investigative link he thought he had now turned into a maze. He no longer knew who was to blame for Becky's death and his doctors death.

He was not sure how far the cult had spread and who was a member and who was not. He feared to probe further because he was now aware that too much probing could lead to death.

Henry could not get Elena out of his mind and he decided to go visit her. He sent her a message and she confirmed that she could meet him at a diner in the evening. Henry got home, freshened up and changed into comfortable clothes and he headed out to meet

Elena. He was still feeling disturbed and needed to relax and release the tension he had. Elena was already at the diner when Henry got there. She seemed quite busy browsing through her mobile phone. "Hello, sorry I am late. I took a lot of time in the shower because I was feeling a bit tired but I am feeling much better now," said Henry as he thanked Elena for waiting up on him. "It's okay dear, I just got here. I was looking up some interesting stuff just before you came in. Want to hear about it?" asked Elena. "Yeah sure. I would love to hear what interested you that much," said Henry, smiling enthusiastically at Elena. She stated narrating to Henry a story she had been reading on the internet about some demonic cults. She explained how these cults initiated members, asked them to offer human and animal sacrifices and in return, they would enjoy financial stability. Henry was glad to find out that Elena was also interested in knowing more about the cult. He decided to talk to her about the recent deaths, his suspicions about Jenese and the death of his previous interpreter.

He narrated everything to her, everything he knew about the cult and she in turn gave him more information about the cult. She explained to him how the cult works and what happens when someone tries to leave the cult. "You see, once a person becomes a member, it's almost like they have sold out their lives completely. You cannot opt out. You must obey orders and you must give the sacrifices requested of you." Elena explained. "And is there a way one can know a member of the cult?" Henry enquired. "The only way to know would be to observe the person you suspect closely. They are more likely to look confused, or under some influence. They cannot account for their decisions or emotions. Some don't even know why they do what they do." Elena explained further.

The explanation given by Elena fitted very well with how Henry thought Mr. Shannon, the widower behaved. At first, he was overwhelmed with grief but after a short while, his mood changed completely. He decided to talk to Elena about it. "I think I have two people to observe now. I can bet that one of them is a member of this cult. I am not quite sure about the other one but he seems to me more like a member." said Henry. "How else would you explain why a widower would suddenly change moods and start celebrating his wife's death? I really don't get…" The waiter at the diner interrupted Henry before he could complete his statement. He was very cautious not to say anything that might sound suspicious to spectators. The two had not had the time to look at the menu since they were busy discussing the cult and the recent death incidences.

The waiter therefore caught them by surprise and they had to make a quick selection of what to order. When they could not decide what to eat, they settled for simple drinks, just to get the waiter to go. Elena ordered for a huge mug of milk shake while Henry ordered for a cold glass of orange juice. She was very curious to hear more of what Henry had to say about Mr. Shannon. Henry did not have much to say about Mr. Shannon since he had only seen him for a few hours. He however shared with Elena the pictorial evidence he had about the cult's practices as well as the progress of the investigations he had been doing. He now had to include Mr. Shannon in his list of the people to observe closely. Elena, being a lover of adventurous activities offered to join Henry in his investigations. "This is an interesting thing and I would like to work with you to find out more. But remember, we are not an item" She said and they both chuckled.

The night was creeping in slowly and the two had to go back home. As Henry walked Elena to her packed car, he sensed that someone was following them and looked back to find Eric closely following them. He was scared but did not want to look weak in Elena's presence. "So, who is the new chick?" Eric asked jokingly, tapping on Henry's back. "Hi cutie? What should we call you?" He asked, trying to reach for Elena's hand. She was not afraid of him and she therefore answered him, introducing herself, "I am Elena, pleased to meet you uuum, what's your name again?" "I am Eric,

Henry here happens to be my good friend. Right Henry?" Eric answered back.

Henry was forced to look for an excuse to get away from Eric. He dragged Elena into the nearest mall he could find and they walked quickly through the mall, pretending to check out stuff in different stores. The soon lost Eric and they walked out. Elena got into her car and drove off and Henry started walking to his own car. Before he got to his car, he checked to see that no one was following him. Now more than ever, he feared for his life, especially after Dr. Yuri told him that Jenese and the other cult members could possibly be after him.

CHAPTER 8

Henry Gets Kidnapped

AFTER ENSURING THAT Elena was at a safe distance from him, Henry now felt comfortable to drive back home. At this point of his life, he felt that anyone who came near him, especially those who knew things about the strange cult were in danger and they could've be killed any moment. He got so distracted by the things that were happening around him and felt helpless. He feared to ask for help from anyone since he did not want to endanger anyone's life. The only thing that crossed his mind was to go and visit detective Williams so he could talk to him about his suspicions about Mr. Shannon. He was however, wondered how he would be able to talk to Williams without seeming too speculative, keeping in mind that Mr. Shannon is William's brother-in-law. Henry had a feeling that Williams would not entertain anyone trying to incriminate his brother-in-law, especially now that his sister was dead and the children needed their father now more than ever. On the other hand, Henry felt that Williams must be more angered by Dr. Shannon's death than he was and would therefore like to dig deep into the truth of the matter. "He would love so much to find out who killed his sister, to make sure that justice is served," Henry thought to himself as he drove to meet Williams. Henry was lost in his thoughts that he did not even notice that he was being closely followed.

When henry pulled over to text Williams to let him know that he was coming to see him, he noticed a black van, with dark tinted windows stopping just behind him. He was terrified and could not think of anything to do to save himself. Then luckily the cars had passed him and henry had sighed so exhaustedly. As Henry drives back home during the storm, he notices a note from his parents that they and his siblings had gone to visit their grandparents for the weekend. Henry sighs with disappointment that they completely abandoned him. As Henry exhaustedly goes to bed, he then gets an awful nightmare that was much worse than what he has been getting over the past couple of nights. It was from that van that he had seen on the drive to home and little later on, before it occurred to him that he should drive off as fast as he could, men in black aprons and masks were already in front of his car, pointing guns at him. They threatened to bring the windscreen down and kill him if he did not open his doors. Henry opened his doors, with his hands shaking. "Get out of the car boy! And don't you even dare scream if you don't want this to be the last thing that comes out of your mouth!" One of the men shouted at Henry. As henry gets up from that loud shatter from down stairs and slowly comes down the stairs with his heart beating so rapidly. Then notices that the lightning had shattered one of the windows. After henry then sighs from the worries and says, "it was just a dream. "He then decides to go for a drive and then later on the drive he stopped on a red light and then he saw the black van in front of him and said "hey, that looks familiar." little did he know it was those exact same guys that came out from the back and had abducted him! They had black aprons and black scary masks with pointy noses. Which looked exactly like the Maschera Dello Speziale then after they abduct him into the van they noticed that Henry was not moving. "What? You cannot hear. Ha ha! We do not speak signs young boy! Get out or I will fix your ears using a bullet." One of the men said as he dragged Henry from the car and thrashed him to the ground. They then dragged Henry into their van and drove off fast, leaving Henry's car on the side of the road. For the first time, Henry wished he could hear. "Maybe if I could hear I would be able to identify their voices and know who they are behind their masks." Henry thought. He however suspected that one of the men in masks was Mr. Shannon. His physical appearance was resembled that of Mr. Shannon so much. Realizing that fear and self-pity would not help him, Henry decided to use whatever he had to help himself. He gathered all his courage and asked them where they were taking him and why they were doing that. All he wanted was to provoke them to talk. He hoped that they would say something that would help him know where they were going.

Henry was right. One of the men, knowing that Henry was hearing impaired shouted, "We are still in Fair Oaks little brother. Can you hear that?" He asked sarcastically. He did not know that Henry could read lips perfectly well. One thing he was sure of was that this man had no reason to lie because he did not think Henry could read his lips through the small slit on his mask, which was intended to give him the freedom to speak. Henry suspected that they would be taking him to the deepest forests in Fair Oaks and having been to the woods before, he started plotting his escape. He was still thinking about how to escape when the van stopped the men jumped out, dragging Henry out with them. Henry looked around and saw an abandoned building. As henry was to learn later, this was an abandoned mental hospital, sitting deep in the forest. He lost all hopes of ever getting out of here safely. He started thinking about all the things he had done in his life, weighing between the good and the bad. He had heard so much about heaven and hell and he wondered where he would end up when his kidnappers finally killed him. One thought he could not get off his mind was how he cheated on Susan with Elena. He felt guilty because even though he knew it was wrong to keep seeing Elena, he went ahead and asked her out.

When everyone removed their masks, his thoughts were cut short by the sight of Mr. Shannon, Jenesse, Eric, Victoria Motaire and another man he had not seen before. They tied him to his chair and did not talk to him for about one hour, as they got their torture items ready and ate their dinner as Henry watched them. They had carried with them takeout meals, which they ate leisurely, knowing that it tortured Henry to just sit there, not knowing why he had been kidnapped. After a long period of silence, Mr. Shannon approached Henry. "Do you know why you are here?" He asked. "We would have killed you without torture, and make it look like an accident but you forced us to do this. Your big mouth can't just shut up, and that is a problem for us." Mr. Shannon continued.

Victoria and Janesse were now approaching, with syringes in their hands. Henry was scared and did not want to imagine what was in the syringes. "Talk! Do not force us to do this and stop wasting our time!" Jenesse said as she asked Henry how many people he had talked to about the cult. "If you tell us what we need to know we will be kind enough to kill you immediately instead of torturing you." The unknown man prompted Henry to talk. "I didn't even introduce myself, how rude! My name is Sunny Verruckt...note where the stress is...or just call me Sunny," Sunny Veruckt continued mockingly. Henry learned later that Sunny was Mr. Shannon's partner, but before was Henry's evil interpreter and was the reason why he moved to America so that he would not have to deal with anymore. Apparently, he was proven wrong. They not only did business together but also shared a lot more. They were partners in crime and they ran an interpreters' club, where interpreters met and discussed how to grow their business by getting new gigs. Janesse was the first one to give Henry a jab, which made Henry feel weak all over. He could not move a hand. "Two more jabs doses and you will be dead. Talk and we might release you alive." Jenesse prompted. Henry could not lift a hand to sign but luckily, he had learned to talk without signing. The thought of death scared him and he had to talk. He revealed that he had talked to Detective Williams and that they had found the murder weapon used to kill Becky Malone. He however did not reveal anything about Dr. Yuri and Elena. He feared that they too would face the same fate as Dr. Shannon. He consoled himself that William could defend himself and that even if he did not tell them about him, Mr. Shannon would because he was aware that his brother-in-law was helping Henry. All this time as Henry talked, Eric was looking at him attentively, as if he expected him to say something more.

Eric had seen Henry with Elena and even though he did not know Elena that well, he knew that Henry did not go out to meet Elena for nothing. He approached henry, holding a bucket in his hands. He enquired to know about Elena and what she knew about the cult. When Henry did not answer, Eric forced henry's hand through the small opening on the bucket's lid. Henry screamed as ants bit through his flesh. "Yes! Yes! I told her all I know!" Henry screamed in pain. "Good boy!" Eric said while getting out Henry's hand and giving him an evil grin. "But she doesn't believe it. She laughed it off and we therefore didn't have much to discuss." Henry continued, hoping that they would leave her alone. "Good. That is how it should be. We only need people who believe you." Victoria intercepted. "So how about Susan, what does she know? She does not believe you too. Is that why you are already cheating on her?" Victoria prompted further, laughing sarcastically.

All this while, Mr. Shannon was sitting silently, waiting for Henry to say all he knew and who else knew what he knew. "So we have Mr. Williams to follow for now. Interrogate the boy further. I need to go back to my children. C'mon Sunny, let us leave him to his friends. They know what to do." Mr. Shannon said leaving Jenesse, Victoria and Eric to torture Henry into giving out more information.

CHAPTER 9

Sunny Verruckt

SO MUCH HAD happened to Henry in one night. He did not understand why everyone he knew or at least thought he knew chose to turn against him, especially people like Jenese and Sunny. Sunny had been Henry's interpreter in 7th grade. Henry never liked Sunny at all from the very beginning. He was one of Henry's worst interpreters and in fact, one of Henry's reasons to move to America. Henry was surprised to find out that sunny had moved to America too. Sunny and Mr. Shannon had met at the interpreters' club and they became good friends. His own father introduced sunny Verruckt to the cult, after he demanded to know where his father always disappeared to on weekends. After learning about the cult, he was scared that his own father would sacrifice him one day. To avoid that, he decided to join the cult. He believed that this would give him immunity against any evil plans of the cult. Sunny grew arrogant as he continued to follow the cult's practices and even now, he cares about no one. All he cares about is expanding the cult and cutting down any negative publicity against it. One of his greatest achievements was to introduce the cult in Tokyo, Japan, when he visited on a holiday trip. He managed to get a few faithful followers, who he commissioned to grow the cult community in Japan. When he found out through Mr. Shannon and Jenese that

Henry was digging into details about the cult and that he had information that could incriminate some members of the cult he was determined to do anything to stop Henry. From his experience, Sunny knew that Henry was very aggressive when he decided to do something. He knew that if they did not stop Henry, they would be risking a lot.

Back at the mental hospital, the night was long and cold for Henry and he could not wait for it to end. With the kind of torture he went through earlier that night, he was not even sure that he would survive through the whole night. He was a bit relieved when Eric and Victoria had to leave, leaving Jenese alone with him. He somehow hoped that she would lose sight of him so that he could try to escape. Jenese was however not going to let Henry escape. She gave Henry a larger dose of the injection she had given him before. He immediately fell unconscious, giving Jenese time to take a nap. Henry remained unconscious for some hours, after which he regained consciousness. Realizing that he was all alone in the dark room, Henry tried to free his hands from behind the chair, where Jenese had tied him. He felt a piece of stone using his feet and tried to reach for it, toppling over his chair.

After an hour-long struggle, he managed to reach for the piece of stone and started cutting the rope using it. After a while, he managed to free himself. "Freedom at last! Henry thought to himself as he searched for an opening through which he could escape. He went to the door and tried to open it but it was barred from outside. He finally found what he thought was an alternative way to the outside. He broke a window and sneaked through it. To his dismay, he found that he had only managed to enter another room. This room was however larger and had several corridors leading to different parts of the hospital. Each corridor Henry walked through thinking that it would lead him outside led either to another room or to a dead end. He could not tell how he was brought in here or whether he came in through a door or a tunnel. All windows, which had an outside view, were barrier with a steel grill. He kept walking around, trying to find a way out. He would open each door he found, even if it led to another room, just to make sure that he did not miss a chance to escape.

At the end of one of the corridors, henry found a staircase, which wound down to the basement. He thought that he went down to the basement; he might find an opening to a tunnel, which he would use to get out. At the end of the staircase, there was a tiny door, which opened into a dimly lit room. Henry gently opened the door and stepped in. "Look who's here" Henry felt someone tapping on his back. He looked back to find Jenese standing behind him, with her, a group of people Henry had never seen before. Among them were four men and two girls. They all grinned at him like psychopaths. "We looked for you everywhere…we were worried that you got lost. You know this is not a place for everyone. Sorry we were not here to orient you." Said Nick, one of the people who were with Jenese. They all burst in laughter and seemed to enjoy watching Henry swallow the bitter reality that he was never going to get out of that place.

"He is kind of cute," said Diana, one of the girls who were with Jenese, as she removed her belt. "Let's know what to call him boss," She continued, lightly stroking Henry on the neck. "Come on, give me a smile honey. What? Don't you like me?" she continued jokingly. All this time Jenese sat and watched. Henry could not stop his tears. "Poor boy! He is already desperate…see how he is crying like a baby." Jenese said as she approached Henry. "Treat him well Diana and I might consider gifting him to you." Jenese continued as she invited Diana to the tease Henry. He was not expecting it when Diana started whipping him using her belt. He felt a sharp pain as the belt's buckle landed on his back. "Think we are here to entertain you? You owe the boss information and may will only stop when she had what she wants from you" Diana mocked Henry as she continued whipping him. The others just stood there, cheering and hooting after every whip Henry received and encouraging Diana to whip harder.

"Don't you understand that he will be of better use to us when a live than dead?" Mr. Sunny asked as he walked in, startling Jenese who was enjoying watching as Henry screamed in agony for his dear life. "I thought you had a plan to get us the information we needed? How will killing him help us here?" Sunny continued, feeling disappointed that the group was only enjoying beating Henry up without prompting him to talk. "Careful Sunny, I think this boy here can perfectly read your lips. You don't want him thinking that we are divided or that his life is that important to us." Jenny intercepted before Sunny could stop Diana from beating up Henry. She beckoned Diana to stop beating him and Mr. Sunny picked him up, sat him on a chair and tied him up again. "Tough guy huh? I hear you managed to untie yourself?" Sunny criticized Henry. "I want to teach that you shouldn't escape from home...wait... you don't even know that this is your new home. Do you?" Sunny continued and the whole group laughed, chanting, "Welcome home! Welcome home!"

Mr. Sunny went back to the van and brought cups of coffee he had bought on his way there. After distributing to his friends, he teased Henry with one cup of coffee but when Henry refused to accept it, Sunny poured the hot cup of coffee on Henry's head. "You don't like coffee? Sorry I did not know...either way, this coffee this coffee is yours. You will still take it" He said as he poured it on henry's head. "Oh look! He was thirsty. See how he drinks well with his hair. Ha! Ha!" Sunny continued to mock Henry. He groaned as the coffee burned his head and dripped down to burn the fresh wounds on his back. "So, tell us something about that other doctor. Mr. Shannon mentioned to me that you were seeing another doctor. What do you have to say about her? Or do you need more coffee to re-energize before you can talk?" Sunny threatened to pour more coffee on his head.

Henry could not stand more pain and he blurted out a name, which he made up to protect Dr. Yuri. "Her name is Dr. Julia! Please promise me you won't hurt her," Henry said, trying to sound as desperate as possible so they would not suspect that he was lying. "You don't make demands here!" Tom, one of the young men who had accompanied Jenese warned, giving Henry a hard punch on the face and another on the gut. "Don't die yet; we are not done with you." Jenese said as she helped him back to a sitting position with the help of Mr. Sunny. Henry had ran out of tears and he just sat there, staring blankly at his kidnappers. He could not even begin to comprehend why Jenese was doing that to him. Among all the people who were there torturing him, he thought he knew only Jenese better. He was almost sure that they would kill him because there was no way they were going to risk his being out there, knowing that he had seen them and he could easily sell them out. One thing Henry had sworn to himself was that he would not risk any life for his own because he felt that he had already lost it. As the people left one of the supervisors threw a plate with a piece of bread and said "eat and get some rest you're going to need some energy for tomorrow or whatever is left of it" he leaves laughing sinisterly.

CHAPTER 10

The Hunt

ON THAT SUNDAY evening, Henry's parents came home to find that he was not home. They were a bit worried because he had not been communicating with them all the weekend and when they tried his phone, they could not reach him. When they did not find him home, their worries escalated and they decided to seek help from the police if he did not come home by nightfall. It was not Henry's character to come home late and therefore, when the time reached 10.00PM and Henry was not home yet, his parents drove to the nearest police station to record a statement. The police were a bit hesitant to help them. They demanded that the parents come back after 48 hours of trying to look for Henry. "Our son has been missing since the weekend and you are asking us to wait for another 48 hours before you can declare him missing?" Henry's father shouted at the officer in charge. "How many times do we have to clarify that we have not heard from him for the whole weekend?" He continued shouting, feeling agitated that the police officers did not consider their case serious. "Calm down Sir. When did you say you travelled?" another officer intervened, trying to calm Henry's father down. "On Friday evening officer." Henry's father replied. "Okay, so you believe that your son must have went missing since Saturday?" The officer asked. "I believe so officer. Please do something about it. "My son is hard of hearing and he needs al help he can get. Please do something!" Henry's father desperately begged the officer. "I understand your predicaments sir. The law requires us to wait for 48 hours before we can declare a person missing. However, it does not forbid us from helping you seek your son before the 48 hours are over. If you believe he is in danger, then we might be able to help you find him. Tomorrow morning we will be to declare him missing and have all police stations around Fair Oaks notified of his case so they too can help to find him.

Detective Williams walked in just after Henry's parents left. He was curious to know who they were and what they were coming to report. "Poor guys, they lost their son. They said he is hear of hearing and begged us to help them find him" One of the officers explained to William. "What did they say is the name of their son?" Williams asked. "He is called Henry. They went on a trip on the weekend and on return, they found him missing." The officer replied. Williams gasped when he heard the name Henry. He remembered seeing Henry's message on Saturday and wondering why he had not shown up after he had sent him a message saying that he was coming to see him. Williams is not the paranoid type of people and he therefore did not think that anything bad could have happened to Henry when he did not show up. "We sent his parents' home to rest while we try to dig into whatever we can to locate him." the officer continued to explain, realizing that Williams was not listening. "We need to track his car. I know his plate number. The boy had been helping me with the case of Becky Malone's murder and the last time we talked, he was driving to meet me. He said he had something to say about my sister's murder." Williams intercepted. "If we can find his car, we can trace where he went from there, or who took him from his car. I believe so because his car has a dashboard camera. Let's hope against hope that those who took him didn't know this piece of information." Williams continued. When Becky died and

Henry was able to connect her death with the evil cult, he did not feel safe and he had a camera installed in his car. This was done with the help of Detective Williams and only he and Williams knew about it. Williams promised to always look out for him and protect him from the bad people, but in the case where he was not able to do so, he would get evidence to make sure that anyone who hurts him ends up in jail. The camera was intended to gather evidence of every place where Henry visited using his car.

Back at the abandoned mental hospital, Henry's kidnappers were planning on how to keep him in their possession for long enough to be able to get all the useful information from him before killing him. Mr. Shannon was busy with his sons, now that their mother was no longer there for them. Eric and Victoria had classes to attend the following morning and they too could not be there. Jenese and Sunny were therefore the only people left to "look after" Henry, or rather, to torture him into giving up information. "From the way I know Henry's parents, they must be looking for him." Sunny explained to Jenese. Sunny had known Henry and his family long before they moved to America and he knew how much his parents cared about him. "So what do you suggest we do?" Jenese asked. "We can leave Henry with some of your "soldiers" and go out there and stop anyone who tried to come our way," Sunny suggested. "No! These idiots will kill him before he give us anything. They enjoy killing...killing slowly. By the time we return, he will be dead and all our efforts will have borne no fruits." Jenese explained, declining Sunny's suggestion. "I was thinking that we should call a crisis meeting. We should all be here planning how to avoid being caught. We cannot have others running their lives normally while we are stuck here," Jenese suggested. The called back Mr. Shannon, Eric and Victoria to come back to the forest so that they could plan a "hunting mission" together.

"If we could hunt down Henry's parents, detective Williams and both of Henry's girlfriends, we could stop them from hunting us. I believe they are our greatest threat and if we wait for them to come at us, they might get us." Jenese explained to the group when the others arrived. "We are not going to kill them because that would raise alarm. We are just going to point them to another direction." Jenese continued. "I am currently Henry's interpreter and his parents still trust me…" "If that swine did not tell them what's going on yet!" Eric interrupted. "We will have to gamble with that for now." Jenese said, hoping that Henry's parents still trusted her. The plan was to find Henry's parents and Detective Williams and make them think that people from outside the town abducted Henry. Jenese would try to convince Henry's parents that she saw the men who took Henry and that she followed them until she could not follow them any longer, fearing for her own life. Eric would look for detective Williams and sell him the same story. They believed that this would lead them far away, from where they were and it will clear them off all suspicions. The gathered that if they too were missing, they would be the first suspects if Henry is found dead later. Sunny and Mr. Shannon would be left to watch over Henry and try to get more information from him without killing him.

The team dispersed to take care of their assigned duties. Jenese made the first move. She called Henry's parents and asked them whether they had seen Henry anywhere over the weekend. Not knowing the truth about Jenese, Henry's father explained to her that they returned and found that Henry was not home. Jenese lied to them that he had seen him with some people and that they drove off to some unknown place. She also lied that she did not notice any form of resistance from Henry and for that reason, she assumed that Henry was safe and did not call to inform his parents. She also promised them that she would come to see them the next morning to help them continue to look for their son. Detective William was fed with the same story by Eric but he was not going to buy that story. Not until he had found Henry's car and confirmed that indeed Henry drove off to another town. Their search had yielded minimal results. They had only managed to find the last location where Henry's car was on the roadside. They had not however not managed to find who took it from there and where it was driven. They were however determined to search for his car and had found a few leads to finding it. According to the report the other police officers shared with the Williams, Henry's car was still in Fair Oaks and they were expecting to know the exact position where it was come the next morning.

CHAPTER 11

Finding Henry

HENRY WAS NOT sure what day it was or even what time it was. His only hope was that the gang kills him but leaves his family and friends alone. He knew that when his parents returned, they would try to search for him and feared that they might end up being hurt. He could not stand the thought of his own father and mother being in his position, being tortured and humiliated. He was in the worst condition anyone could ever be in. Unlike Jenese who was kind enough to let henry go for nature calls, Mr. Shannon and Sunny did not allow him to do so. They instead humiliated him when he begged them to allow him to go for a nature call. "Hold it in boy! If you can't hold it any longer you can as well go where you are. It's no big deal." Sunny said, giving Henry an evil grin. They forced him to eat some badly cooked soup and bread which Mr. Shane said was meant to keep him alive for as long as they wished. "You are not dying today boy… not yet. We are not yet finished with you." Mr. Shannon said as he forced henry to eat the worst meal he has ever had.

Henry's parents went back to the police station very early in the morning to find out what the police had done so far to find their son. They found a little hope when Williams broke to them the news of having found Henry's car. Williams and his colleagues had been trying to locate Henry's car the whole night and they were able to find it in the early hours of the morning. The footage retrieved from Henry's dashboard camera revealed how henry was dragged out of his car and into a black van. It however did not help in the identification of his kidnapers since they were all in masks. "I think you should know this before we set out to look for Henry. His interpreter came to us earlier last night claiming to have seen henry." Henry father explained to the police how Jenese had lied to them, something which according to him raised suspicions. The policemen were surprised at what Henry's father had just told them because they too had heard the same story from Eric. "Well, that's not true as you can see from the video. And that tells us something…in fact, it can serve as a good lead." Williams said, with his face suddenly brightening up. "This can only mean that both Jenese and Eric know where Henry is and they only wanted to misguide us so we won't find him easily." Williams continued, happy that he had already found his first suspects. "We should fetch those two first before we do anything else. Let them record their statements and explain why they lied to everyone." One of the police men suggested.

Jenese did not plan to go back to the mental hospital until later in the afternoon. She wanted to observe what the police would do with the information Eric had given them. She thought that Henry's parents believed her and therefore, she did not worry about them as much as she worried about the police. When the police knocked on her door, she was startled because she was not expecting their visit. She quickly rushed back to her room, dropped her pajamas and picked a towel, tying it loosely around body. She then walked to the door and opened the door slowly, with a smile of her face. "Who honors me so much this to pay me a visit in the morning?" Jenese asked as she winked at the police men standing at her door. "We are here to talk about Henry. Heard that he is missing? What do you know about his whereabouts?" One of the policeman asked, ignoring Jenese's seductive look. "Come on in please...what will you have? Coffee? Tea? Juice? Me?" Jenese asked, while giggling in a seductive manner. "We are not here to play one of you silly games girl! Get some decency!" the other policeman shouted at Jenese, feeling offended that she would think that her seduction would make them lose focus. "You talked to Henry's parents yesterday night about Henry. We are aware that you lied about seeing him drive out of town and we will need you to come with us to the police station" He continued. The police men took Jenese with them after giving her a minute to dress up. Both Jenese and Eric were thrown into a police cell where two police men manned them while others went out to search for Henry.

At the mental hospital, things were getting out of control. Henry had not yet regained consciousness from the previous night and Mr. Shannon and Sunny were worried that he might die, which was against their plans. Jenese had instructed them not to allow him to die because according to her, he would make a great sacrifice to "the high god" after they were done with him. Jenese kept reminding the team that cult practices did not allow them to kill someone who had been promised to the gods and now they could not risk letting Henry die. They tried reaching Jenese on her phone and when she did not answer, they sent her a text message, asking her to return to the mental hospital as soon as she could.

"I think we have a message for Jenese" One of the policeman said, holding Jenese's phone in his hands. Both Eric's and Jenese's phones had been taken away by the police officers who hoped that something positive could come out of it. "Here, it says...are you listening Jenese? This message is yours." The policeman said, poking Jenese with his staff. "Where are you? What is going on out there? Please come back as soon as possible. All is not well on this side" He read out loud. "ZZZZZ! ZZZZ! ZZZ!" Jenese's phone vibrated as another message came in. "Oooh, another one!" said the policeman.

"It says, he is having convulsions! Come soon or at least tell us what to do! I think the last dose we gave him was too much for him" The police officer continued reading out loud. "Someone call back or the search teams. The search is ended. I think we already have our person here with us." Detective Williams ordered as he dragged Jenese from the police cell. "You are going to lead us to the exact place where you have kept Henry" Detective William ordered, addressing Jenese. "Make this easy for us and your punishment might be relaxed a bit. If you make it hard for us then you will have to suffer the full consequences of your actions." Williams said, probing Jenese to lead them to the abandoned mental hospital where they had Henry. "And don't even try being clever…we already tracked where your messages were coming from and we will still go there even if you don't lead us there." William continued.

Mr. Shannon and some of Jenese's "soldiers" had been out spying when they noticed the police officers and fled away, leaving Sunny and Diana alone with Henry. Mr. Shannon tried to send a message to Sunny to inform him that the police men had raided their hideout but the message could not be delivered. Henry did not even realize when the police officers stormed the mental hospital, rescuing him and arresting Sunny and Diana, one of Jesse's psychopath friends. He woke up in a hospital bed, confused and wondering how he had managed to get out the death pit he had been thrown into. When he woke up to his mother's smooth caress, he almost jumped out of bed in fear, thinking that it was Diana who was playing her dirty games on him. "Shhhh, calm down dear…it's me…your mother…calm down" His mother soothed him, trying to get him back to sleep. "It over now son." His father joined in to sooth him. Henry laid his head down, thinking about all what had happened to him and thanking God that he was still alive. He was however more worried than relieved. He was happy that Jenese, Eric, Sunny and Diana had been arrested but he was also not stupid enough to think that

that would be the end of it all. He had seen Jenese's "soldiers" and he knew what they were capable of when they were angry. He also did not underestimate Mr. Shannon and the fact that he was still out there and free made a cold sweat break from his forehead. Henry was careful not to scare his parents with all this information. At the same time, he was careful not to disclose to them any information that would place his parents in danger. His thoughts were cut short by the sight of Susan. "I was worried sick about you! "Thank God, they found you! She cried as she leaned to give Henry a hug. Susan had grown anxious waiting for Henry to be found. She could not imagine losing him and now she did not want to let go of him.

CHAPTER 12

The Park of No Return

A T THE HOSPITAL, Henry was having a hard time sleeping, even though the doctors had recommended him to have a good rest. He would wake up from his sleep in the middle of the night and start screaming while calling out the name of his kidnappers, asking them to spare him or kill him quickly. His mother who never left his side all the time was so much worried that Henry would develop a permanent psychological problem due to the trauma he had been through. She remembered Henry telling her about the evil cult and their practices but she ignored him, telling him that those were just rumors spreading to instill fear in people. She did not want to imagine what could have happened to Henry if the police had not intervened in time. Henry's mother was distracted from her deep thoughts by his father's voice, "how is he doing? You really need to go home and take a rest. You need it." He said as he walked in, offering to look over Henry so that his mother can go home and rest. "No dear, I have actually been waiting for you so that we can go and see Detective Williams. He had earlier requested to speak to us both." Henry's mother objected. "Susan offered to stay with him while we talk to William. Remember her? The girl who came here yesterday...she said she was very close to Henry." She continued. As they were talking, Susan came in, allowing them to go and see Williams.

William's office was not very far from the hospital where Henry was hospitalized and it took Henry's parents only minutes to get to Detective William's office. "Thank God you are here! I almost thought you were never going to come." William greeted Henry's parents. "I called you here to talk about what Henry had told me some time before he was kidnapped. Please make yourselves comfortable. This could be a long story," Williams continued. "Thank you Williams, I don't think we got the chance to thank you enough. We owe you so much for our son's life." Henry's father said before taking a seat next to William's desk. "It's nothing sir. Henry has been helping us with a case of two murders and he deserves all the help and protection from us, As William pours a glass of wine on both glass cups and offers one to Jim and Karen." Williams said as the parents sit on the couch. "Actually, that's why I called you here. I wanted to tell you more about what henry had told me and what I found out after digging further." Williams Continued. "Henry is actually very lucky to be alive. They must have had a special purpose for his life to keep him alive for all this time." William continued, without any intentions to scare his Henry's parents.

William explained how Henry came to him after Becky's death, seeking help in finding her killer. William had been reluctant to buy Henry's story but he was also curious to know more about the cult. Henry's story reminded Williams of a case he had handled several years back, when he was very fresh in service. It was about a man who had been killed and left by the roadside by a strange animal. "Has Henry told you anything about what he saw at Creek Village?" Williams inquired. "I only heard him talk about the death of his interpreter and saying that it was linked to an evil cult and that she was offered as a sacrifice to the 'gods' of that that cult. I did not follow up so much because I thought it was just one of the scary stories he liked reading from the internet." Henry's mother replied. "Before all this happened, Henry told me that he had heard about the cult and had been following up to know what it was all about. Last Halloween, henry and some of his friends had gone to creek village, intending to have fun and scare each other. What Henry told me he saw there was very close to the case I am talking about? He told me that he saw an old looking man pull a girl from the crowd and disappeared with her into the thick forest. He never saw that girl again." Williams explained to Henry's parents. "I remember that day. Henry came home looking tired and scared. He could not sleep that night but he refused to say what his problem was." Henry's father said, looking surprised that their son would keep such a secret to himself. He even wondered how much more he knew and what the cult members would have done to him if he had not been found in good time.

"Well, that's what he told me he saw. In addition, it reminded me about this case, of a man who was killed and left on the roadside by a strange animal. According to the witnesses we interviewed, the man was driving when he noticed an old man trying to cross the road. He slowed down to allow the man to cross but he started approaching his car. The driver pulled over and got out of his car, intending to help the old man. As he stepped out of his car, the old man pounced on him, biting him and sucking blood from his neck. He did not have time to scream for help and even if he screamed, no one would dare come to his rescue out of fear. When he lifted his face, the old man had changed from being a man to a scary looking animal. His face was starting to grow far and it was filled with blood. His eyes became narrow and they turned blue. Everyone was fleeing away screaming and the animal fled away into the thick forest, taking with it the poor man's head," William narrated to Henry's parents. "Oooh my God! Has all this been happening here or did you forget to say you read it from a book? Henry's mother asked, looking terrified and shocked." From that time, Creek Village had been feared." Williams continued.

"Are the rumors I hear about the place true?" Henry's father asked. "I once heard that deep inside the forest there lived some blood drinking creatures and they only came out to hunt when they are hungry." Henry's father continued. He remembered having heard the story Detective William had just told them and ignoring it as a rumor. Creek Village had earned itself the name "The Park of No Return" since it was rumored that all those who went there never returned. Henry' father was even surprised to hear that his son actually visited the park and came back alive. The only reason why Henry came back alive could have been that he had not gone deep into the forest. "I cannot really tell the truth in that story but from what I have seen and heard, I have all reasons to believe they are not just rumors. I am now convinced that these creatures do exist and that they somehow are connected to the cult Henry was yelling me about." William replied. "We will be investigating the suspects more. I believe that they are behind every murder that has occurred in the recent past. Meanwhile, I need you to be vigilant and report any suspicious activities you see around you or anything henry tells you." Williams said, dismissing Henry's parents. "Okay sir. We will report anything we see… but please do us a favor and protect our son… promise us that nothing will happen to him again." Henry's mother begged Williams.

Having arrested Jenese and her team, William was positive that the murder of Becky and Dr. Shannon would be solved. He, however, did not know that there were some more people who had escaped. He also was not aware of the danger that loomed for all those who knew about the cult. Mr. Shannon and the rest of Jenese's soldiers were angered by the arrest of their friends and were already preparing to rescue them and avenge the embarrassment caused by the police. When Williams went to visit Henry in the hospital, he did not get a chance to talk to him about the cult and the members who were arrested and what had happened when he was kidnapped. He also understood that Henry was suffering trauma from the previous events and he therefore did not want to increase his troubles. What Williams did not know is that by not talking to Henry, he had made the gravest mistake of his life. If he had talked to Henry, he would have warned him to be more careful and reinforce his security since some of his kidnappers were out there and they were looking for anyone with incriminating information regarding the cult. It only occurred to Williams that not all was over yet when he returned to his office to find a picture of a skull placed on his desk. Not even the secretary had an explanation of where the picture had come from.

CHAPTER 13

Jenese Escapes

THE POLICE CELL is no place for a girl, especially one who had never imagined herself behind bars all her life time. Jenese's arrest was the worst thing that ever happened to her and she was determined to escape before she was taken to prison. She knew that there was no way she was going to win the case. She was accused with two counts of murder, and one count of kidnapping and intended murder. While in her cell, she kept quiet, meditating her escape plan and her revenge once she was out. On their first day in court, Jenese met Diana, Eric and Sunny and communicating to them in their secret cult sign language, she told them of her plan to escape. The four were going to play their little nefarious game. Then their case went on and once their verdict was given, they would execute the plan.

Before the second hearing of the investigators had planned to investigate all the suspects and trick them into giving up information about the other members, especially those who had a lot of influence. "I understand that you were only being used to execute your commander's orders." One of the investigators started, while investigating Jenese. "If you tell me who your commander is then we promise you to relax your sentence. Now look at it this way, you are still very young and if I guess right you do not have children yet. If you go to prison now, your name will be forgotten as well as your existence." The investigator continued, trying to sound emphatic. "Why do you care if I am remembered or forgotten?" Jenese asked rudely. "Do with me whatever you want to do with me. It will be a great honor to die in the service of my god." Jenese continued with a snare on her face. "I wouldn't call it think of it as an honor to suffer or die for someone who wouldn't do the same for me. Name them and let us see what they are going to do for you. Has any of your commanders come to see you since the time you were arrested?" The investigator continued, hoping that this would make Jenese talk. "Never trust any crazy ideas you get about me. What makes you think I have a commander?" Jenese asked, looking at the investigator in the eyes. "All right, I will give you time to think about it. Meanwhile, remember that, they will never die for you." The investigator said as he walked out leaving Jenese alone.

Eric, Diana and Sunny too were not ready to give out information. Sunny even went ahead and threatened the investigator by telling him that even if they killed him, the investigators would be hunted down and taught a lesson or their life if not killed. His arrogance was not helping the case since the investigators took that as a serious threat and added it to the cases Eric was supposed to answer in court. The second day in court turned out to be the last day of the case. The four suspects were all lined up in one big chamber from where they answered the prosecutor's and the lawyers 'questions. They had no hopes of getting a good lawyer and they therefore accepted a state lawyer to represent them. "When Mr. Shannon entered the courtroom, they did not notice him, apart from Jenese, who had been expecting Mr. Shannon to show up with a 'lawyer'. The prosecutor was surprised by the new turn of events. He had never worked with this new lawyer nor had he heard of him. He wondered what would make him so good in mind r cases if he wasn't all that experienced.

The prosecutor, the judges and jury were later to learn that this so-called lawyer only came as a prop. As the prosecutor read out the cases the accused were there to answer to, the four-started nodding in unison and when he finally shed, they all pleaded guilty. This turned out to be the shortest murder case ever. "Are you agreeing that you killed Becky Malone and Dr. Shannon?" one of the judges asked. Seeming perplexed. "Yes, we are! What will you do about it?" Jenese replied back harshly. One of the court officers pulled Jenese from the chamber, so roughly that she hid he head on the wall. "We will make sure you pay dearly for not only the murders but also for disrespecting the court. "The officer said, forcing Jenese into a police van. The other three were roughed up too and throw into the police van. They were being transferred to different prisons and the ladies were to be dropped off first before the men could be taken to their prison.

Just a few miles from the town, the van's driver almost lost control of the van after he drove over a spiked chain, which had been buried in the dust road leading to the women's prison. He was able to bring the van safely to a stop and he stepped out to check what had happened. The policemen who had accompanied the prisoners too stepped out, locking the prisoners in the van. They were lucky to find that only one tire had been punctured by the spikes. As they were preparing to change it, another car pulled over close to the van and out came 6 men, all dressed in black aprons and masks that had a picture of a skull. They were fully armed with guns and they started shooting at the police officers. There was a fire exchange which took place for more than thirty minutes before all the policemen and their driver went down. The men in masks took the van's keys and opened for Jenese and her team, releasing them to freedom.

"That was brilliant Jenese! I never imagined it would work out but I chose gamble with it because either way, I was doomed already"

Sunny said once they were comfortable in the car. "I told you to trust me. No prison will ever see me...not when I can still think and when I have people like Mr. Shannon and Mr. El Dorado. Jenese replied, bragging about her success. El Dorado was the prop lawyer who had shown up at the court. His duty was to find out which van they would be transported in and to follow it while communicating to others to set up the trap ahead on the dust road. "Those idiots will have a hard time catching us because they will not know that we escaped until after several hours. They will only notice when we do not get to our respective prisons at the expense expected time. This will give us enough time to flee the town." Jenese continued, rolling out her plan to the others. "Where are you planning to take us from here boss?" Diana asked. "I was thinking about West Sacramento. We can find several friends over there. But we are not going until we have taught everyone who crossed our path a lesson. We will also risk being caught if we try to escape today. We are therefore going to lay low until everyone has given up on finding us." Jenese continued to explain.

Henry was first on the list of people who were to be punished by Jenese. He did not know this yet because he thought they were already in jail. His biggest worry was to get the rest of the cult members arrested and sent to prison too. After a week of staying at the hospital, Henry was discharged and he needed to talk to his school principal to explain to her what had happened and how some students had become dangerous for the school's safety. He knew that the principal already knew this and thought that it wouldn't be so hard discussing the matter with the principal. That morning, he woke up feeling uneasy. He didn't know why he was feeling so but he needed to go see the principal since schools were almost back in session. He asked Susan to accompany him and while they were driving there, Susan kept complaining about how it was a bad idea for them to be out alone especially after all what happened and after the police had confirmed the escape of the four wheelers had been arrested.

Susan's fears were confirmed when they arrived at the school. There, at the main entrance of the administration block was their principle, tied to a pillar, and with Fresh blood still oozing from her throat where the knife cut through. Her eyes had been plucked out and her fingers and toes too cut. The police had already arrived at the scene and had secure the area as a crime scene. Henry and Susan were not allowed to go near the scene, but they instantly understood what had happened. Jenese and her team must have assumed correctly that once Henry was discharged, he would want to come to the school to talk to the principal. He believed that they did this to teach him a lesson and to give him a warning that they would still be coming after him.

CHAPTER 14

The Investigation

VERYONE HENRY KNEW and trusted was dying in the hands of Jenese and her gang. It was almost as if Henry was being haunted. After finding ng his principle tied to a pillar in front of her office, Henry gave up his quest to have Jenese taken to prison. He feared that the next person he thought of talking to would die too. Still, he could not get off his mind the thought of what they could do to all the people he was talked about when he was kidnapped. He was worried about Williams but even more about Janet. He could not live with himself if anything happened to Janet, all because he could not keep away from her when he should have. The death of his school principal hit him very hard because it was unexpected. Of all the people, Henry did not think that the principal was going to die. He hated himself because he believed that he was the reason why all these people were being killed. The investigations of the principal's murder were very complicated since the only suspects were nowhere to be found. The police now concentrated on protecting all the people Henry had mentioned to them that needed protection. Although Henry had vowed to stay away from the investigations regarding his school principal's murder, he could not help but notice that Williams was not actively seeking involved in the investigation too. He always found reasons to avoid meeting Henry and Henry though that he was only doing this to protect him. He had no idea that William's life was in eminent danger too.

Williams had received several threats after rescuing Henry. Every day he would find a picture of a skull on his desk and sometimes a sticker with threats on his car. He could not solve the puzzle of who dropped the pictures and the stickers, when and how he/she did it unnoticed. He thought of all possibilities, including black magic and when he could not find an answer, he decided to lie low, keeping off all investigations shortly and ensuring that he was always secure. He was desperate to catch Jenese and her team and take them back to prison but he could not do that with his safety already threatened. He needed to wait until a time when they were unsuspecting then he would catch them. Williams advised Henry to keep off the investigations for a while. He was not to go out by himself or with someone who could not protect him. With Henry and Williams silenced, Jenese and her team got the chance to escape from town unnoticed. They were aware that if they tried to fly out, they would be caught at the airport. The plan was to take a train to West Sacramento, and then they would connect from there to Los Angeles, where they would stay for a while. Jenese had promised them that she would get them accommodation with some of her friends, who were members of the cult too. The four spend two days to get to Los Angeles. With a bounty placed over their heads, they did not want to risk booking a hotel room. They spent the nights on the streets and in the mornings, they would try to change their appearance to avoid being noticed easily. Travelling by train came with an added advantage because the trains stations were usually crowded, enabling them to travel without being noticed.

Los Angeles was the perfect place for the four to take a rest and hide from the police. This is a city that received so many visitors and noticing new faces in the city was almost impossible. Back at

Fair Oaks, they knew that people like Mr. Shannon and the other members of Jenese's gang were safe because no one suspected them to be involved in all this. The only people who seemed like a threat to Shannon and the others were Henry and Williams but they had made sure that they silenced them before escaping. Jenese had several friends in Los Angeles, most of whom were members of the cult. She took Eric and Mr. Sunny to one of her friend's house who had offered to live with them for a short while Jenese and Diana lived with Jenese's cousin. "You guys are going to live here for some days before we plan what to do next. This is my good friend El Dorado." Jenese said, welcoming Eric and Sunny to El Dorado's house. "I remember you from somewhere!" Eric exclaimed. "Yes, we met I court, and later on your way to prison. I helps set you people free. Now you are here! You owe me so much already." El Dorado said jokingly. "But you do not have to pay anything. All thanks to Jenese. Since she is so loyal, I am always loyal to her." He continued, showing Eric and Sunny their respective rooms. "You will stay with them for some time just like we planned. Right?" Jenese asked. "Of course! Of course! Anything for you sweetheart." El Dorado reassured her. "Alright, you guys take a rest. We meet tomorrow morning for breakfast." Jenese said waving the people good-bye. "And make sure they take a shower El Dorado! Those two can really stink when they want to." Jenese added jokingly as she left.

The next morning while they shared breakfast, Jenese and her friends discussed their recent predicaments. What could have caused them? "The gods must be angry with us." Sunny said when no one seemed to have an answer to why all of a sudden his or her secrets were being exposed. "We have been running our practices quietly for some time now until the death of Becky. Do you think we were wrong to kill her?" Eric asked. "No! Never regret anything you did in the service of the 'highest god'." Jenese warned. "I had warned you earlier Jenese not to expose the activities we do in secret. However, you were so arrogant to listen. It would have been better if people thought that Becky was just missing and would be found eventually." El Dorado said, expressing his disappointment in Jenese's idea of exposing Becky's murder for the world to see. He felt that none of this would be happening if the gang had continued with their practices in secrete. "You see the reason you can find a hide out here in Los Angeles is because we have not exposed ourselves for the world to see us and know who we really are. Do not get me wrong. That does not means we do not offer sacrifices. We do offer sacrifices but not without thinking of the consequences. Every person we wish to disappear has to disappear completely." El Dorado continued. "It's Okay El Dorado...I know the drill already...we need clean up the mess behind us...ooh...and we need to stop leaving traces...what else? Almost forgot! Next time you will not be there to help us. I got it already. I messed up and I am sorry. I came here so we can perform a cleansing ceremony. We need the god's protection now more than ever." Jenese said, cutting El Dorado short before he could finish his statement.

The cleansing ceremony was supposed to take place at The Point Reyes, which is approximately six hours from Los Angeles. The beach along The Point Reyes is rocky and foggy most of the time. It therefore served as a prime location for the cult's activities since not many people visited the beach, especially during the cold season. On this particular day, the beach was so foggy that one could not see anything beyond a hundred meters. For the Cleric, Diana, Jenese and Sunny had to offer a human sacrifice to the gods. They were to look for young girls, preferably not older than 16 years and bring them back to The Point Reyes, where they would be killed and their blood applied on the foreheads of the four to signify their cleansing. After arriving at The Point Reyes, the four took a short rest and went out to hunt for young girls to offer as sacrifices later in the night. They approached the clearer parts of the beach, lured young girls into following them. They would later forcefully carry them to an abandoned asylum near the beach, knowing that their parents would not see them once they disappeared in the fog. At the wee hours of the morning, the gang was preparing to leave the asylum when they heard a creaking sound on the stairs. They could hear footsteps from far and as the footsteps got louder, the creaking sound got louder too. They all stood in different positions, holding knives in their hands, ready to attack whoever was approaching. When the door opened, Sunny exclaimed in joy. "Sam Putnick? Is this you?" Sunny dropped his knife and ran to greet his old friend Sam. "This is Sam Putnick, an old friend and one of the first people I got introduced to when I first joined the cult." Sunny explained, introducing Sam to the others. "I figured there were some people here because I thought I saw some light. I came here to warn you that the police sometimes come up here to check see if anything fishy is happening here. Come let's go to my newly discovered hideout." Sam said, while ushering the group to an abandoned shipwreck on the shores of The Pointe Reyes.

CHAPTER 15

Sam Putnick: The Canoer

SAM PUTNICK'S SURPRISE entrance startled everyone in the team. Most people did not know him, including Jenese but he knew them all by names. He knew Jenese, Eric, Diana and Sunny and where they had all come from. Only Sunny knew Who Sam was and why he was there. "Hi all? Do not be scared. It is my duty to make sure that all my brothers and sisters are safe around this beach. Once I identify that you are one of us, I have to make sure that you are safe and that you will not be easily caught." Sam introduced himself. "Sunny here can tell you how we met and how we knew each other. I am not surprised to find new faces here because there are several people who have come to know this place and we allow them to use it because we understand their need for a hidden place." Sam continued. "Come on Sam! Enough with the speech! First, how have you been? How did you find us?" Sunny interrupted.

"Should we be worried about being caught here? On the other hand, how easily did you know there were some people here? Sunny enquired. "Okay, the thing is, the police are already suspicious of the recent deaths that have been happening around this beach. They are searching everywhere and all I can say is that this place is not safe at all." Sam replied. "Come; let me show you a better place where you can be sure that nobody will dare looking." Sam continued, leading them to the opposite direction. The group walked for a while before getting to a place where a shipwreck was left behind. This wreck turned out to be the best hiding place for the group because it was far from sight. People could not see it from the beach and it was between huge rocks, making it even harder to see it. All this time, Jenese was tensed. She did not know whether it was a good idea to trust Sam but since Sunny had insisted that he was a good friend and that he was the one who showed him the asylum, she had no option but to trust him. Sunny and Sam seemed to get along very well and this comforted Jenese very much.

Sunny had visited The Point Reyes on several occasions while looking for a lone place to perform his rituals. When he first discovered the abandoned asylum, he was pacing along the rocky beach alone, looking for a perfect place to offer a sacrifice to the gods. He had only been introduced to the cult and was required to give his first sacrifice. For the sacrifice, he had identified a very young girl, probably in her early adolescence. He had been cautioned that he had to offer a sacrifice that is very pure and therefore had to look for a girl who was still a virgin. He however did not know of a safe hideout where he could offer his sacrifice and go undetected. While he was walking, he felt a tap on his shoulder. A young man had been following him silently, seeking to satisfy his curiosity about who Sunny was and why he was walking on the lonely and rocky beach alone. Sunny was reluctant to talk to him and he increased if pace. The young man called out as Sunny disappeared to the thick fog. "Hey! If you want, I can take you around the beach with my canoe. I know places over here. People say that a lot goes on around this beach, but I fear no such things." Sam Putnick said to Sunny, offering to help him. This was how Sunny and Sam's friendship began. Sunny had not told Sam exactly what he was looking for, but it was as if Sam already knew whom he was and what he was looking for. Sunny did not trust him but he needed help finding his way around the beach.

He followed Sam slowly, but did not agree to board his canoe even for a second. As they walked, Sunny noticed that Sam had a weird tattoo on his left arm. He could not clearly tell what the tattoo looked like, but he thought he saw a bull's head. Knowing what it meant, Sunny decided to ask Sam whether he knew anything about a secret cult. Sam had already seen Sunny's tattoo and it was for that reason he was trying to help him. "These tattoos are very important. They are not just a sign of a pledge to the "high god" but they help us recognize each other easily. I saw your tattoo and though that you must be fairly new in this because your tattoo was too much in the open." Sam said to Sunny when he realized that Sunny did not trust him. He led Sunny to the abandoned asylum and showed him a secret entrance through which he could use to get in if he came in alone. The main entrance was barred tightly to prevent anyone from getting in and only people who knew the secret entrance could get it. It was here where Sam Putnick and a few other cult members came to perform rituals and offer sacrifices. They would later throw the bodies out into the lake, making it look like the victim had drowned in the ocean. Sunny became good friends with Sam and he has to meet with a few other cult members before he moves to Fair Oaks to meet Jenese and the others.

When he was not fishing, Sam Putnick was a Canoer. He used to take people around the beach in his canoe and sometimes, across the narrow bridges. He found Canoeing perfect for him because he could easily get from one point of the beach to the other easily, canoeing between the rocks. Sam had been acquainted to most parts of the beach and he knew the safest and the riskiest places to perform a cult ritual. He also had an easy time getting his target victims. All he needed to do was to trick them into to getting into his canoe and then taking them to abandoned parts of the beach, where he would kill them and offer them as sacrifices. Later, he would throw them into the water. He had discovered the shipwreck when he was taking his victim to a lone place. While avoiding being canoed too far and came to the point where the ship had been left. From then, he had been going to perform hos rituals there and had intended to reveal the place to other cult members who would need a hide out too.

For the cleansing ritual, Jenese and her team had to offer a virgin girl to the 'high god' and vow not to expose the secrets of the cult again. They had already kidnapped two young girls from the beach and were going to kill them, draw some blood from them and dispose of their bodies before going back to Los Angeles. Just as they entered the abandoned ship, the group heard gunshots from a distance. Police sirens too could be heard coming from the abandoned asylum. "We would be dead meat right now if it were not for you Sam." Diana said, thanking Sam for his kindness. "You don't know what you just did for us. We would either go back to jail if caught or even be killed" Diana continued. "Not back because were never there in the first place. Eric interjected. "What happened, why were you in going to the jail? Sam asked. "Oooh… we didn't even tell you. We almost messed up big in Fair Oaks. We almost exposed all our activities, and everyone is looking for us to send us to jail." Jenese replied. "That's why we came her to be cleansed. El Dorado sent us to the abandoned asylum where you found us. Jenese replied. "Who? El Dorado? You trust that person. He must have been the one called the police in for you. In addition, the police were never going to arrest you. They would have killed you all instantly." Sam said, looking rather worried. "Don't say that about him. That man saved us from going to jail!" Eric interrupted. "He did, but because he wanted to bring you here. To kill you all so he can contain the rumors before they spread too far. Don't you people get it? That is how he keeps the cults secret from spreading around here. If you become a liability, he kills you!" Sam explained. I would suggest you do not go back to him. He already knows that you were not caught at the asylum and he is not pleased. I would advise you to stay away from him. Just make sure you don't cross his path." Sam Continued. "No. He should make sure; he does not cross our paths. Hell, he already did! He will have to pay for this." Jenese replied, feeling disappointed that her friend would betray her so much.

CHAPTER 16

The Revenge

A FTER REALIZING THAT they had been played by El Dorado, Jenese and her team planned on how to make him for trying to get them killed. "The Point Reyes is no longer safe for us and nor is Los Angeles. We will therefore go back to Fair Oaks and teach everyone who tried to hurt us a good lesson," Jenese said to the group after they were done performing their rituals at the abandoned shipwreck. "That sounds good Jenese. We will not keep running forever. We have to show these people that they should never mess with us again." Eric said, agreeing with Jenese. The team spent a few days with Sam Putnick, where they were acquainted to the team he used to work with. Sam had a lot of influence at The Point Reyes. He had a team of serial killers who he used when he needed to go to war with some people. Sam's team was made up of four men and one woman all who had various crime histories. The men were also involved in money laundering and they had created a very complex network of people who could help them get from one place to another. Juliana, the only woman in Sam's small team was an expert hacker who helped the rest in evading the police by erasing all their police records. At first, Jenese thought that she was too slender and did not seem like someone who could take care of herself. She did not approve going to 'war' with her because she felt that it would be an added liability. However, when the team was planning, her contributions amazed everyone, making them realize that they needed her as much as they needed each other, if not more.

Juliana cautioned them against going back through the same rout they had used to come there. "Think about it, the police must be looking for you up to now. In addition, if they gave up their active searches, it means that they have beefed up searches at airports and train stations. They probably know where you traveled to and how." Juliana explained to the team, suggesting that they needed to use a bus to go back, however slow it might seem. "We need to see what the police system has about you. We can easily make your records disappear to avoid being caught at police checks." Juliana added. Her plan was to hack into the police system and erase all the records the police held against Jenese and her friends. She knew that even if they were taking a bus, there was a chance that a police officer would stop them and ask to check the bus. If the police did not have their records, it would be hard identifying them. With this plan, the team would safely get back to Fair Oaks, where they would execute their revenge plan. First on the revenge list was El Dorado. Henry would be next because according to the team, he was very weak and could not defend himself. They felt that it would be very easy getting back at him. Following Juliana's advice, the team arrived back at Fair Oaks. Jenese gathered her own team, which had been left under the care of Mr. Shannon. Together with Sam's team, the group was big enough to attack El Dorado and his team.

On a Friday, evening after the team had confirmed the whereabouts of El Dorado's team, they a few were sent out to tail El Dorado and capture him. It was their expectation that once they had El Dorado, his team would come looking for him and that way, they would attack, killing all his 'soldiers' and finally kill him after torturing him for some time. El Dorado loved staying indoors and this made it quite hard for the team to get him. After a few hours of waiting at his driveway, the team was lucky to see him walking out. Immediately after he drove off, they followed him closely. They did not allow him to go too far from his home when they attacked. They first shot at his wheel using a silenced gun, bringing his car to an immediate stop. They forced him to open his car, threatening to kill him if he did not. El Dorado opened the door and walked out slowly. "You will regret this! You do not know who I am. I would advise you stop doing this when you still have the chance." El Dorado threatened his abductors in hopes that they would let him go. "Shut your big mouth and get into the car. You don't give orders to us!" One of the people said to El Dorado, thrashing him to the ground and tying his hands behind. The team threw him into the car and drove off to the deep forests of Fair Oaks. They kept him there for the rest of the night, torturing him as they had planned and forcing him to call his team to come to his rescue.

Just as planned, El Dorado's people came running to his rescue, not knowing exactly how many people they were coming to deal with. Before the team could get to the point where El Dorado was held captive, they were met with gunfire. Jenese's team had secured some long-range shooting guns in preparation for the fight, putting El Dorado's team at a disadvantage. By the time they came near their rivals, a few members of El Dorado's team were down already. One mistake Jenese and her team made when they were planning their revenge mission was to assume that El Dorado had a small team of weak people. They were shocked when El Dorado's people kept coming at them, and the numbers did not seem to reduce significantly even after they had killed several of them. Things started changing when Juliana went, and Sam Putnick went down. Sam's team felt that Jenese's team was not doing as well as expected and that they only concentrated on protecting Jenese and her close friends, Eric and Shannon. This gave El Dorado's team an advantage which saw several of Jenese's 'soldiers' brought down.

The gunfight, which was expected to go for a few minutes. Before all of El Dorado's, team members dismembered. went on for quite some time, attracting the police to the scene. There was a lot of confusion when the police arrived because all the two teams were against each other and against the police too. When they saw the police officers, Jenese, Eric and Shannon fled into the deeper parts of the forest, leaving behind their teams to fight the police. Williams noticed Jenese and her two friends fleeing and started following them. Before he could get too far into the forest, a few Jenese's soldiers who survived the gunfight caught up with him. Thy shot at his car, bringing down the windscreen and all the car windows. After killing the officers who accompanied Williams, they took him captive, promising to deliver him to Jenese so she could kill her personally. When William tried to resist, they knocked his head on a tree trunk, rendering him unconscious. Before they could throw him into their car, other police officers ambushed them, killing them all and rescuing William. The police officers took him to the hospital, where they learned that Williams had gone into a coma and that he had suffered a brain injury, which could lead to amnesia.

Jenese, Eric and Mr. Shannon too did not go too far before the police caught up with them. They managed to arrest Eric and Mr. Shannon but Jenese managed to escape. Left alone and not being sure how much time she had left, Jenese vowed to take revenge on Henry by herself. "It is because of Henry that all this is happening." Jenese thought to herself. She was convinced that if Henry had not started digging into the death of Becky, then they would never have been forced.to abduct him and the police would never have known the truth about the cult and its practices. "I now know what to do. I will hot hit where it hurts most. I will take both of his girlfriends and make him choose between them. If he does not, I will kill him while they watch then kill them one by one. No one messes with me." Jenese thought to herself. Now that she was a lone and she knew that the police were looking for her, she planned to track both Elena and Susan during the evenings and catch them one by one. The news of the killing of the evil cult's members helped Jenese in her plans because everyone was now feeling secure and free to walk out alone in the evenings. Elena and Susan were not suspecting it when they were kidnapped. They found themselves together in and an old abandoned building, not knowing why they were there and why their kidnapper asked them questions about Henry. Susan painfully found out that Henry had cheated on her with Elena when Jenese mockingly started calling them co-wives.

CHAPTER 17

The Reunion

JENESE SEEMED TO be in no hurry to call Henry to come and rescue his girls. He wanted him to suffer looking for them and then make him suffer even more watching them die of he did not cooperate. This particular evening, she seemed to be in a good mood. "Today is a good day for me and one of you, whoever Henry chooses. He might choose you honey. Oooh how beautiful" Jenese while reaching to caress Elena's face. Elena spat on her face in disgust and looked away from her. "Go to hell! You will not get away with this. Not this time." Elena said. All this time, Susan was crying silently. She paid no attention to what Jenese said because it was hurting her more than any physical torture Jenese could give her. Jenese brought the girls to a long dinner table and cuffed their hands behind their chairs. She chose a horror movie for the girls and went to the kitchen to prepare dinner. "Today we are having a small party then we will play a little game afterwards. Moreover, let no one disrespect me by turning away from the screen. I want you two to enjoy the movie or else I will slit open your throats." Elena said while grinning wildly and pointing a knife at the girls. She started preparing dinner as she watched the girls struggling with fear. "Have you seen where that girl's eyes are picked and removed with a fork yet? That is my favorite part! Can you imagine what I can do with you? Oooh we are having so much fun today!" Jenese shouted from the kitchen as the girls screamed in terror. "Quiet please! Do not ruin my dinner mood! Quite!" She shouted again, furiously walking towards the girls. She pulled a gun from one of the kitchen drawers and carefully placed it on the dining table. "Anyone else scream again and I will blow your brains off your pretty head." She threatened as she walked back to the kitchen.

When she was done, she set the table, served her meal and served the two girls. As she sat to eat, she texted Henry, asking him to come and rescue his girls. "I got your girls here with me and they seem so rude. Please come for them. I can't deal with them." The text message read. After receiving the message, Henry forwarded it to Williams, who had already recovered from the injury he had sustained. Williams and a team of SWAT officers started planning how to attack Jenese when she least suspected. "You go ahead so she won't realize that we are coming. Don't take too long on the way because she will know that you were planning something." Williams's texted Henry back while he and his team were getting ready for the attack. They understood that Jenese never worked alone but they were also aware that most of her soldiers were dead and she would not therefore have enough back up when they attacked.

When Henry walked into the Mansion, the sight of Susan welcomed him and Elena sitting at the long dinner table, with their hands cuffed behind their chairs. At the far end of the dinner table was Jenese, comfortably enjoying her dinner. She slowly raised her head as Henry entered, picked her gun and pointed Henry a seat using the gun. "Hey! Thanks for coming. Dinner was almost getting cold. Have a seat and join us at please." Jenese said to Henry, trying to piss him off. "You will regret this Jenese. I swear to God your will. Henry said to Jenese, seeming irritated. "Let them go or both of us will die here today." Henry threatened. "Relax Henry. We are only playing a game." Jenese said to Henry. Henry became enraged and tried to attack Jenese but before he could, two men rushed and pushed him away. They pulled a chair away from the dining table, made him seat and tied his hands behind the chair. "Okay. Now that it seems you have decide to calm down, let's start the game." Jenese said to Henry. "The first steps of the game are very easy but it gets complicated as we play on. So brace yourself." She continued teasing Henry. Henry could not bear the sight of Susan's tears. Every time their eyes met, Henry would drop his face down as he avoided looking at her. His worst fears had been confirmed in the worst possible way. He always feared that Susan would one day come to know about his encounter with Elena but he never thought that this would be the way she would find out.

"Okay. Let us start here, when did you meet Susan? What about Elena?" Jenese asked, "That's none of your business." Henry replied. "You think so? I am sorry to inform you that actually it is. Make it faster and safe them all." Jenese replied. "Okay! Do not hurt them please. I met Susan first. Is that enough for an answer?" Henry said, pleading with Jenese to stop the sick game. "Good. So you are admitting that you payed Susan? Poor thing! Now tell Susan what happened with Elena." Jenese continued. "Nothing. Nothing happened" Henry said, avoiding Susan's face. "But you were going out with her. Right? Jenese asked, placing her gun on Elena's head. "Yes! Yes! Yes! Please do not hurt her! She is innocent of all this. "I like your cooperation. So whom do you love most? I will spare the one you love." She continued. When Henry hesitated, she threatened to shoot the two of them. Henry, who was now scared and wondering why the police had not shown up yet, had no option but to cooperate. "I love Susan! Please do not hurt them Jenese. Please!" Henry pleaded. "I will eliminated one problem for you then." Jenese said pointing the gun at Elena. Just as she was about to shoot, the front door of the mansion was kicked in by the police officers as they flooded in. Jenese's soldiers tried to fight them back to protect her but they were outnumbered. Before she fled, Jenese shot at Elena, taking her down with her seat. She tried to escape from the mansion through a secret entrance but the SWAT team had already covered all the escape routes. After killing all her soldiers, the police officers closed in on Jenese and took her to the police station.

While some of the police officers were following Jenese, others were trying to safe Elena's life. They placed her on an ambulance where two paramedics attended her on her way to the hospital. Henry and Susan were escorted back home by Williams and Henry was left to try to cheer Susan up. Henry could not stop blaming himself for what happened to her and he hoped that one day when she was better she would consider forgiving him. He was also stressed out because all the while, Susan had not said anything to him. "I love you Susan. I do. I don't know what I was thinking cheating on you with Elena." Henry said, trying to start a conversation with Susan. "Say something please. At least react. If you want to hit me hard on the face I will totally understand." Henry begged. "I once told you that I love you no matter what you do. Nevertheless, please tell me, must you do silly things all the time? There will come a time when I can no longer love you Henry. Don't allow our relationship to get there." Susan finally replied. Henry almost jumped up with joy after hearing Susan's words. "Does that mean you forgive me now?" Henry enquired with a wide smile on his face. "Yes Henry. But there will be no second chance." Susan replied. There will be no need for that because I will not waste this chance again. Henry said, Kissing Susan. Amidst all the happenings, nothing could make him happier than knowing that he no longer had anything to hide from Susan and that Susan was kind enough to forgive him. The reunion between him and Susan was one of the best things that had happened to him the whole year.

Henry and Susan were distracted from their moment by the sudden bang on the door. When Henry opened the door, he found

William standing on the pouch. "She escaped again!" William said under his breath. We are trying to run after her. I only came to warn you that you shouldn't go out because she could try to get you again." Williams said. "Keep your phone on please. I couldn't find you on the phone earlier when I tried to reach you." Williams said as he said good-bye. He quickly got into his car and drove away, leaving Henry and Susan in the house scared to death. They were aware of what Jenese could do to them if the police did not find her on time.

CHAPTER 18

Jenese

I F THERE WAS, one thing that Jenese would not allow was being caught by the police. She had vowed to herself that she would not go to prison while she could try to avoid it. When she managed to escape from Williams and his colleagues, Jenese went into hiding, only coming out at night to buy a few stuff from the stores. In order to change her looks, she was forced to dye her hair blonde and change her dressing style. She started putting on excess makeup when she was going out and wearing oversized clothes. One evening she walked into a diner to buy food and noticed that there were posters all over with her photo and a prize promise for whoever found her. She made her order very fast and walked out before anyone would notice her. As she walked down the streets, she noticed several other posters like the ones she had seen at the diner. She walked into an accessories shop, grabbed a pair of sunglasses and wore them hoping that they would completely hide her identity. "I am doomed if anyone notices me." Jenese thought to herself as she waved stopped to get a cab back. She had figured that the police would not look for her at the abandoned asylum where they had found Henry because they would assume that she would not hide there. She was right. The police had spent quite some time trying to look for her but they had not thought of checking that place.

Before Jenese got into the cab, she thought she saw someone who looked like Henry from a distance. She did not concentrate on finding out who it was because this would get her caught again. Henry had not seen Jenese. He was busy trying to find the location of the Diner where they had agreed to meet with Susan. The two had stayed indoors for some time and needed some time together. Although Henry was scared that Jenese might be waiting to abduct them once they stepped out, he still took his chances because he needed to see Susan. Susan's parents had hired her a bodyguard after the ordeal with Jenese and promised her that they would always ensure that she was safe. "Heey Susan! I am glad that you could come. I would have understood if you couldn't make it because I too know that it is dangerous out here especially now that Jenese is still free." Henry said, greeting Susan. "I had missed you so much. I wouldn't turn down our date." Susan replied. "So how do you feel now? I know we have been communicating on phone but I want to hear it from you. Do you still feel traumatized by the encounter with Jenese?" Henry asked. "I don't know how I feel about that. All I can say is that I am angry that she is still free. I mean…is anyone at least trying to look for her?" Susan replied, sounding irritated. "I don't understand how a criminal can go missing for such a long time. For how long are we supposed to wait before we can move on with our lives? I am so tired of being followed around like I am a small kid." Susan continued angrily. "I think the best thing would be to stay out of trouble for now while we wait for the police to do their job." Henry said. "Williams revealed to me that they have already have a plan. He thinks that they can easily find Eric, Victoria and Mr. Shannon and force them to reveal Jenese's whereabouts." Henry explained. "Okay then. I hope that works because I cannot stand the thought of someone dying or anything happening to of us. That psycho must be put behind bars." Susan replied as she looked at the menu for something nice to eat.

Finding Shannon was not hard because he had been pretending to be clear of all involvement with Jenese. He had gone back to living his life, assuming that no one would ever suspect him. Henry had however told William everything about Shannon's involvement in his own kidnapping. The police offered Shannon immunity if he revealed Jenese's location but Shannon did not have anything valuable to tell them. They released him after he promised to help them look for Jenese in exchange of his total freedom. With Shannon's help, the police were able to locate Eric and Victoria. They gave them the same promise they had given Shannon if they could help locate Jenese. Victoria was hesitant to accept the offer. "You are sick if you think I can betray my own mother for a bare promise." Victoria answered back to the police when they asked her to help them search for Jenese. "You can choose to go to prison with her or let her go there alone." The police officer replied. After they left the police station, Victoria thought about the offer she had been given, finding it lucrative. She was tired of hiding all the time and having to pay for her mother's mistakes. She did not see anything see would be losing by revealing her mother is hiding location. "Where is she when I need her the most? She always busy satisfying her sickening desire to hurt others." Victoria though to herself.

The next morning, Vitoria and Eric walked to the police station with a complete plan on how to find Jenese. Victoria was going to call Jenese's secret cell phone number. Only Victoria and a few other close family members had this number. She did not expect Jenese to pick up the call as fast as she did. When Jenese answered, the police were able to track her location. They planned that the three; Eric, Victoria and Shannon would ask to meet Jenese and after she agreed, the police would follow them. "So these idiots have been silent all this time and they think that I would trust them?" Jenese thought to herself after she disconnected the call from Victoria. She agreed to meet the three at the abandoned asylum where they would have lunch.

When they arrived with packed lunch was already at the door to open for them. She took the boxes and set them on the old table. Before they sat down to eat and talk, Jenese excused herself to use the washrooms. After 5 minutes, Victoria suspected that her mother was not coming back. She tried opening the door, only to find it locked and barred from outside. All windows were closed too and there was no way they could get out. "Does anyone else smell gas or am I the only one?" Eric asked, concerned. "Where the hell is your mother? Why are we here and she is not? Why can't we get out?" Shannon started shouting at Victoria. Victoria did not have any answers for Shannon's questions nor did she have answers for her own questions. She wondered what her mother's plan was. She knew that she was a dangerous woman but she did not think that she would kill her own daughter. Shannon and Eric tried opening the door but before they could, the whole building was engulfed in fire. They were trapped in there, without any way out and without anyone to rescue them. By the time the police officers arrived at the scene, the building had been burnt to the ground and Eric, Victoria and Shannon burnt beyond recognition.

Realizing what happened, the police spread out through the forest to look for Jenese before she found her way out. Before long, they were able to find and arrest her. She was taken to state penitentiary where she was locked up as she awaited trial. Her arrest was received with a lot of relieve by Henry, Susana and their families. They were happy that they could freely walk around without endangering their lives. With Jenese locked up and all the other members of the cult dead, the cult was disbanded. She was the only member of the cult standing and did not have anyone to help her escape again. Her arrest also gave Henry the freedom to visit Elena in the hospital. "I am so sorry Elena about what happened. I want you to know that it was never my intention that you get hurt." Henry said, standing at Elena's bedside. "Don't be sorry. You had no choice. I remember we agreed that what happened between us was a one-time thing?" Elena replied. "I remember that but I still feel responsible for your current condition. The good news is that Jenese has now been arrested. She is currently locked up as she awaits trial." Henry explained to Elena. "I want to see her rot in jail just like I promised her." Elena replied. "It's happening already. So will you forgive me please? Can we still be friends?" Henry asked. "Of course…I have nothing against you. We have been good friends and we will keep it that way." Elena said as she laid her head back to rest.

CHAPTER 19

The Verdict

ENRY HAD GROWN quite independent in the hearing world and he no longer needed an interpreter to interact with people. Although he was taking language therapy classes to enable him to read lips better and talk perfectly like a hearing person, his greatest motivation to learn was the negative experience he had had with interpreters. He hoped that he wouldn't ever have to be followed around by an interpreter. Henry was out practicing basketball when his phone started vibrating. Susan was on the line. She and Elizabeth had been out shopping and Henry wondered why she would be calling at that time. "Was she not supposed to be enjoying shopping and trying on new clothes and shoes? I though that's what girls liked." Henry thought to himself before he answered the call. On the video chat, Susan seemed overjoyed. "Hey honey!" She said as soon as she was able to see Henry's face on her phone. "Have you seen the news?" She asked. "No I haven't. Tell me more please." Henry replied. "After waiting for a full year, the court's final verdict regarding Jenese has been given" Susan said, increasing her pitch in joy. "And what's the final verdict, I hope this time it is some reasonable verdict." Henry said on the other end. "The court sentenced her to die Henry. She will be getting 'the needle'…and… the jury is not listening to any other appeal regarding her." Susan continued to explain. Henry did not know how to react to such news. Part of him was overjoyed that justice had finally been served and that the several deaths Jenese caused had been avenged. He did not however think that the best thing would be to kill Jenese. He felt that sending Jenese to prison for the rest of her life would be enough punishment. he even though that it would be better than the death punishment since that would torture her more than death by a lethal injection.

The court's verdict came a great relief to all who had been hurt by Jenese. It had taken a long period of time since her lawyers kept on appealing after each court verdict. The first verdict which was made a few weeks after her arrest was for her to be jailed for life. After a few months of her staying in jail, her lawyers brought an appeal before the court, claiming that Jenese might have been involved in weird stuff like the cult but she was not a killer and hadn't killed anyone. They claimed that if she was a killer, she would have killed Henry, Elena and Susan when she kidnapped them. With this appeal, Jenese was promised to be pardoned after some years, but only if she behaved well in the prison. After some other month's Jenese's case was back in court again and this time the lawyers were asking for her release, claiming that the court and the prosecutorial team had made a ruling marred with prejudice. They claimed that Jenese was a victim of a flawed justice system which discriminated against people based on their race. It was during this final trial when Victoria Motaire appeared in court, surprising everyone including her own mother. No one expected her to show up because everyone though she had died in the fire. When the police officers could not find her body, they declared her dead, assuming that she was burnt to ashes. It was Victoria's testimony in court that made the jury make the decision to have Jenese killed. She broke down in court explaining how her own mother tried to kill her and how she managed to escape. She also revealed how her mother used to kill innocent people while performing her cult rituals. With such revelations, the court was left with no option but to give Jenese the maximum punishment for her crimes, which was a death sentence. Having confessed to being her mother's accomplice in her crimes, Victoria was sentenced to 2 years in prison, after which she would be released and put under parole. Before she was sent to prison, she was allowed to pay her last respects to her mother a form of appreciation for her confessions which helped in ensuring that justice was served.

Later that evening, Henry, Sam, Susan and Elizabeth went to the prison morgue to view Jenese's body. When they got there, they found a team of forensic doctors performing some tests on her body and preparing it for sendoff. It was already late and the doctors needed to go. When they were done, the doctors went out, leaving the body on the table so that all who wanted to view it could do so. As Henry and his friends were going in to view that body, they saw Victoria coming in. They were not sure what to say to her because they knew that she must have been sad that her mother was dead and at the same time relieved that she had paid for trying to kill her. Henry and his team left Victoria to mourn her mother and wen to have dinner together.

"Now that we have confirmed that she is really dead, we can celebrate." Elizabeth said once they were all comfortable at a diner. "Yes! Everyone order your favorite food…and drinks too…and don't forget to pay for it…haha!" Henry said jokingly. "I am buying everyone dinner…seriously now." He added. "You know you are so funny? No wonder I fell in love with you." Susan replied. "Yes yes yes…can we talk about love later when I am full? We can talk about how much we loved the food." Sam said, teasing Susan and Henry. "The past few years have been tough and we never got the chance to talk about love. All we could talk about was safety. So now allow us to talk about love when we can." Susan replied and everyone laughed hysterically, feeling relieved that they could joke about the past few years. Since Becky's death, Henry and his friends had gone through tough times. It had become so hard to even concentrate in school when all one could think about was how Jenese or one of her accomplices would appear from nowhere and abduct them. Security checks at the school gates had intensified and all students had been asked to be vigilant in reporting all cases of suspicious behavior after the principal had been found dead. Now that Jenese was dead and Victoria was under parole, they had no reason to fear. The sect seemed to have died out completely after Jenese's arrest and there was therefore no danger of new people being recruited into the cult to continue Jenese's activities.

"I think we have stayed out for too long. Does anyone remember that next week is the final exam week?" Henry said after noticing that a lot of time had passed after they were all done eating. "Oooh! I almost forgot that I have some papers to study for." Elizabeth replied. They all got up to leave to their respective homes. Being the final year of high school, Henry and his friends did not have much time to spare. They were all determined to excel in their final exams so they can qualify to go to college. Henry and Susan Planned to apply to the same universities so that they wouldn't be separated when they go to college. High school had been great fun for them apart from the last few years when they had to deal with Jenese. Susan could not wait to finish here exams so that she could start preparing for prom. She had long been waiting for it so that she could vie for the prom queen in her year. Her mother had given her a story of how their family had had a history of winning the prom queen title. Her grandmother had been prom queen in her year and so was her mother. She was now determined to win the title to continue her family's legacy. On the following day at school, Susan and Elizabeth spent the major part of the morning sticking campaign posters on notice boards. Susan was not as popular as her competitors on the title but she had a reputation of being kind than all the popular girls in the school. She hoped that her kindness would encourage people to vote for her. She was also planning events that would make her popular by the time prom night came. For instance, she had Elizabeth and few of her friends had planned to hold a car wash event where they would wash everyone's car in the school compound for a small tip. They hoped that with this event, Susan would become more popular and that she would earn some extra coins to boost her campaigns. She was confident that come prom night, she would be crowned prom queen and she hoped that Henry would change is mind as time goes by and compete for prom king.

CHAPTER 20

The End

EXAMS WERE OVER, and everyone was busy preparing for prom. For Susan, prom was a big deal because she was hoping to win the prom queen crown. She had managed to get Henry to agree to compete for the prom king position, but she had noticed that he was not serious in his campaigns. To popularize herself and Henry, Susan organized a fundraiser at which they sold snacks. They would later use the money collected from the fundraiser to buy some food and new clothes to donate to charity. Susan wanted to emphasize on her strengths of being kind and charitable. She hoped that with such a positive image, winning wouldn't be so hard for her. Looking for the perfect dinner gown for the prom night was also a challenge for her. Most girls in the school had already bought their dresses and were showing them off in pictures but she had not decided on the perfect dress. The night before prom, she went to visit Henry to know what he would be wearing so that they could go in matching clothes. She learned that Henry had not been seen since morning and his parents had tried to reach him without any luck. A lot was running I Susan's mind then. "What could have happened to Henry? Could he have been abducted again? And who could have done that this time? I thought Jenese was dead?" Susan questioned herself silently. She did not want to break down before

Henry's parents and so she had to leave them and pretend to be okay. She drove back home feeling disappointed, angry and worried at the same time. She tried calling Henry's phone several times on her way back home, but she couldn't reach him. She did not even bother to go to the stores to buy a gown since she saw no point in buying a dress when she didn't have a prom date.

Susan parked her car and walked fast to her house, she was already worried about Henry and scared that something bad might happen to her too if she was out for too long. She opened the door to find Henry and a group of her friends comfortably seated. They all looked at her as if there was nothing odd about them being there at that time and without her knowledge. "I have been trying your phone since morning Henry! Where have you been? Who opened the door for you?" Susan asked angrily. "Your mum." Henry replied shrugging. "So why were you not picking your calls?" Susan asked. "Calm down and be my prom date my love. Did you think I was going to assume that you will automatically be my date without me asking?" Henry replied, grinning at Susan. "I had already given up when I couldn't reach you. I don't even have a dress." Susan replied. "Go to your room Susan." Henry said. "She doesn't trust you any more Henry." Tristan said, laughing at Henry. In her room, Susan found a nice silver dress on her bed. She remembered going to the stores with Elizabeth some time back and seeing a dress like this one. She admired it but thought it was too expensive for her to afford. "So Henry went through all that trouble to get me the dress that I like?" Susan though as she tried on her dress. "It fits perfectly." It was Elizabeth this time. She was standing right behind her with her own dress.

"How did you get in? How many of you are here? You guys are scaring me." Susan said, laughing lightly. "Don't you like the surprise? Henry really loves you Susan. Never forget that." Elizabeth replied. After trying the dresses, the two changed and walked downstairs to join the others at dinner. They did not want to show everyone what their dresses looked like since "that would spoil the glam" according to Elizabeth. Prom night was even better than expected. She enjoyed dancing to the slow music with Henry. Winning the prom queen title was the best thing that happened to Susan all her high school years. She now looked forward to her graduation and joining college. Everything seemed to be working well for her. She had secured a place in the same college as Henry and she was glad that they wouldn't need to part ways.

The group had arranged a big party after their graduation. Tristan had earlier earned a football scholarship and would be going to college immediately after graduation while the others waited for a while before joining their respective colleges. Tristan's parents had agreed to give Tristan the permission to hold a party at the house. Apart from Henry, Susan, Elizabeth and Ben, he had also invited several other friends from his class. A few days later, he was on his way to college. Ben had decided to join the army while Elizabeth was going to join the medical school. Susan and Henry were joining the same college after a month to study law. They all agreed to meet again during the Christmas holidays to revive their friendship.

After one year of being apart from each other, the group met again during the Christmas holidays. They all had a lot to share about their lives in college and their new cities. They found it quite interesting to hear about what the others were doing and how their courses were like. Elizabeth told the group a lot about medical school, how the human body works and how diseases find a home in a person's body. Susan and Henry had shared a lot about law too. They also revealed to the others how strong their relationship had grown and that they planned to marry immediately after college. Although the group met severally for lunch, they hadn't gotten the chance to hold a big party like the old days. They planned to hold a party on Christmas Eve and this time Henry was going to host a party at his house. Henry had a lot of shopping to do for the party. It was winter already and Henry expected people to start coming in very early to avoid the snow storms which usually started in the evening. He also expected them to stay there till the next morning. He needed extra blankets for all who would need to sleep. He also needed enough alcohol for everyone in attendance. As expected, people started arriving very early for the party. Henry had placed an order for takeout pizzas and as people walked in, they were handed a box of pizza and a drink of their choice. Henry had planned to engage Susan on this party. At the middle of the night, Henry stood and called for everyone's attention. "Among you all one of the most special people I know. I have been privileged to spend the better part of my life with her and I would like to spend the rest of my life with her." Henry started. Everyone cheered as Henry called Susan to him. He went to his knees and with the most beautiful ring, he asked Susan to marry him. Everyone screamed in joy "Say yes! Say yes!" Susan could not believe her eyes. She knew that Henry was quite doing his best to make their relationship work but she did not expect this. People kept shouting and pushing her to respond until she said "YES".

The party went on well for the better part of the night until something unexpected happened. Someone rang the doorbell. When Henry went to open the door, he found only a huge box at the doorstep. It was addressed to him. He picked the box up, curious to find out what was in the box. He placed it on the dinner table and started opening it carefully as everyone watched. Henry almost fainted when he found William's head inside the box. With shaky hands, he replaced the box cover. Everyone at the party was scared. They all understood what that meant. It could only mean someone was back to continue what Jenese had left unfinished.

Henry thought about Victoria but did not believe that she be the one who did that because she couldn't do it alone. "W a mistake. We did not watch Jenese's send off. If there was any." Elizabeth said, seeming more frightened than everyone else. "You remember that Jenese had this rare disease called *Lupus*?" Elizabeth continued. "Yes." Henry nodded. "But what does that have to do with what just happened?" Henry asked, looking confused. "I learnt from Med School that Lupus reacts to antibiotic and viruses. After getting the lethal shot, Jenese must have woken up later due to Lupus' reaction with the chemicals." Elizabeth explained. "If she did wake up then we expect her to be more dangerous than before. She won't fear anything. Not even death since her brain will not be working perfectly like it would if she had not received the lethal shot. If we…" Elizabeth had not finished to explain when they heard people screaming from outside. They walked out to find that one of the girls they had invited to the party had been taken away by Jenese. She was alive, stronger and more dangerous. Becky Malone.

ecky Malone says as he wakes up Henry "Henry wake up! your
v interpreter is here!...."

e
s
le
ost
ing
red.
that
d.
could
e made